Written on Her Heart

Written on Her Heart

ALAN MAKI

BROADMAN
& HOLMAN
PUBLISHERS

Nashville, Tennessee

© 2002 by Alan Maki
All rights reserved
Printed in the United States of America

ISBN 0-8054-2488-1

Published by Broadman & Holman Publishers
Nashville, Tennessee

Dedication

Joyfully with love,
to Redford and Liz Maust,
my dear friends.

Acknowledgments

I wish to thank my wife Sharon and our children, Shaylan, Shaun, and Mark, for their loving support and encouragement. Thanks to my parents, George and Joyce Maki, for their joy over my successes. Dr. T. E. and Nell Ross gave me time at their guest cabin for my writing retreats at the Pretty Basin Ranch in Darby, Montana, for which I am grateful. And thanks to the U.S. Army and the thousands of firefighters who bravely fought the intense wildfires of 2000 throughout western Montana and other sites in the nation.

Mark Hoselton helped me with pertinent terrain information, and Doug Banks aided me with information on flying airplanes. Doug Nichols of Action International Ministries gave me an insight concerning Romans 12:1, which I used in this story.

Heartfelt thanks to Chris Kingsley, Bitterroot Valley singer and songwriter, for permission to use the words to his wonderful composition, "A Little Piece of the Kingdom." Thanks, too, to Vicki Crumpton for her invaluable assistance and friendship. Thanks especially to Janis Whipple, Kim Overcash, Heather Hulse, Paul Mikos, Pat Fields, Mary Beth Shaw, Lynn Taylor, and all my other friends at B&H who treat me so kindly and do such good work.

Thanks to all my friends at Bethany Baptist Church in Gunnison, Colorado, and First Baptist Church in Darby, Montana. As always, the greatest thanks is extended to the Lord Jesus Christ for his divine guidance through the Holy Spirit during the writing of this book.

Table of Contents

CHAPTER ONE

Drawer of Treasures

Lightning struck the tallest tree on Gash Peak, a lodgepole pine, snapping off several branches and stripping the trunk's bark all the way to the ground. An empty eagle's nest dropped forty feet into the smoldering grass at the root base, sending burning embers into the air. Most of the debris floated harmlessly, snuffing out before settling back down. But one ember, larger than the rest, ushered a tiny flame into a smattering of dry sticks.

Spooked by the crash, a mule deer buck, its antlers in velvet, moved quickly down the ridge and away. The infant fire, fed by a forest that had not known rain for months, insidiously began consuming the undergrowth, spreading its tentacles in search of greater fuels.

"You just got here, Steph, so don't bring up my love life, or lack thereof. At least not tonight."

Stephanie Kline stood in her lifelong friend's backyard in Victor, Montana, admiring the sunset over St. Mary's Mountain and the Bitterroot Mountain Range on the southwestern edge of the state.

"I'm sorry, Molly," she said. "I just wondered if there's anyone new in your life?"

Ignoring the question, Molly Meyers looked to the red-streaked sky. "I'm glad God painted such a pretty picture for your first night."

Stephanie sighed. "Me too." She had flown from Detroit to Big Sky Country earlier in the day. Molly had picked up Stephanie at the Missoula International Airport and driven the forty miles down the valley to her two-story, wood-framed house. The two women had talked the afternoon away in the kitchen, finally stepping outside for a stroll on Molly's ten wooded acres as the sun went down.

"I wish I could bottle this moment for my students back home," Stephanie said, flashing a pearly-white grin. "These mountains and cool night air would go over big." She wrapped her thin arms across her chest and shivered. "Brrr, it's getting cold."

Molly chuckled. "From eighty degrees down to forty. Typical in July around here."

Stephanie, wearing shorts and a T-shirt, gave Molly's loose sweatshirt a tug. "Let's go in and thaw out my goose bumps."

The two friends, both brown-eyed brunettes in their late forties but looking like winsome thirty-five-year-old twins, walked past Molly's two cars in the paved driveway to the rear of the house. They went inside. Eyeing the two suitcases she had left in the foyer, Stephanie abandoned the thought of plopping herself down on a couch, opting to take care of her luggage instead.

"Upstairs, as usual?" Stephanie asked, presuming she would follow the routine of the past three summer vacations at Molly's house.

"No," replied Molly, "take my room. It'll be easier on you."

Stephanie rolled her dark brown eyes. "Oh, yeah, my poor old broken back. Really, it's fine."

Molly picked up Stephanie's suitcases and shook her long hair away from her face. "I talked to Phil while you were flying, and he said you still have some problems."

Stephanie sighed. "He's a worrywart."

"Follow me!" Molly started down the hallway to the master bedroom. "Next time you waterski and fall, Steph, remember to let go of the rope."

"Very funny." Stephanie swatted Molly's shoulder. "Just a buckle fracture. Not that serious."

Molly entered the bedroom with Stephanie at her heels. She dropped the suitcases beside a queen-sized bed.

"There you go," Molly declared, facing her friend with her hands on her slender hips. "You've got your own bathroom, and feel free to use the phone on the table. *Mi casa es su casa.*"

Stephanie gave Molly a hug, then Molly left to prepare a snack while Stephanie unpacked.

After emptying the suitcases and making a mound of clothes on the bed, Stephanie heard Molly call from the kitchen, "Go ahead and use my closet and dresser, Steph!"

"OK!" Stephanie hollered back. She scooped up some socks and nylons from her pile and took them to the oak dresser. She opened the top drawer, found it half full, and tucked her things inside.

When she opened the second drawer, she got a surprise. The drawer contained no clothing at all, but was packed with all sorts of keepsakes and odds and ends.

Stephanie's eyes jumped from a few pieces of jewelry, a small coin collection, and a Girl Scout patch to a child's drawing of a pony and some old ticket stubs for the 1990 Goodwill Games. A lock of blonde hair was sealed inside a plastic bag, some undeveloped film was shoved in back, and an old black-and-white photograph of a family lay beneath two colorful stones.

Filled with curiosity, Stephanie reached into the drawer. She fingered her way beneath some newspaper clippings and old report cards and found two used train tickets to Kansas City. Digging a new path, she found a pile of papers that she squeezed between her thumb and forefinger and worked to get out of the drawer.

The papers were yellowed and had a faint, musty smell to them. The first sheet was dated September 6, 1970, and included only a handwritten poem. Stephanie realized she should obtain Molly's permission before going any further.

"Just one," Stephanie whispered. "What will it hurt?" Her eyes raced down the page.

Watching your plane maneuver,
glittering under night lights,
wings spread like a giant eagle
ready to sail,
taking you away from me.
I still taste our last kiss
as the thing crawls down the runway,
then dashes,
then climbs up, up, up . . .
Crazy red and white and green lights
wave good-bye, good-bye.
I watch, my nose pressed flat
against the glass
until you are no longer a dot,
no longer a speck,
but completely disappeared
and gone,
leaving me alone to watch
other planes coming in,
making believe they're yours.

At the bottom of the tattered page was penned, "Love, James."

Stephanie's heart pounded harder. She knew the author was James Wade, the man with whom Molly had fallen in love in college.

"Steph!" Molly's voice made Stephanie jump. "Come get your tea!"

Stephanie shoved the papers back into the drawer, aware of the trembling in her hands. "Coming!" She shut the drawer, took a deep breath, and headed for the kitchen.

"Have a seat," Molly said as Stephanie entered the peach- and cream-colored room. "I've got chocolate chip cookies and almond-flavored tea."

Stephanie sat down in a pinewood chair as Molly brought teacups and saucers to the table.

Eyeing her friend, Molly declared, "Steph, you look like you've seen a ghost!"

Stephanie put a hand to her pallid face. "I think I have," she muttered.

"What's wrong?" Molly set a full cup of tea in front of Stephanie.

Shaking her head, Stephanie said, "I'm sorry, Moll. I . . ." She almost confessed to her snooping but chickened out. "I'm just . . . I guess I'm tired." She clumsily picked up her cup, spilling some tea in the saucer.

"Watch out, it's hot," Molly warned, taking a seat.

Stephanie gingerly took a sip. "The flight and time change and everything . . ."

"And higher altitude!" Molly said. She took a peek at her silver-banded wristwatch. "I'm the one who's sorry for keeping you up so late. It's midnight, Eastern time."

Stephanie took a cookie from the dessert plate and bit into it. "Not a problem. We've got tons of catching up to do and only a week and a half to do it!" She licked her lips. "Mmm, that's good. Homemade?"

Molly smiled. "Just the way you like 'em! What are friends for?"

"For aiding and abetting a weight gain!"

"Ha! As if it would hurt you. What do you weigh, Steph, about a hundred and thirty?"

Stephanie had shoved the rest of her cookie into her mouth. She took a drink of tea, which burned her tongue. After a howl and a wipe of her finely-chiseled chin, she began laughing.

"A hundred and thirty was five or six years ago!" Stephanie said as the color returned to her cheeks. "If you'd come back to Michigan, we could help each other regain our youthful figures."

Molly smirked. "There you go again, wanting me to move. Last summer you waited a few days before twisting my arm."

"OK, OK. It's just that we're getting older and time's shorter."

"Sounds like you're twisting my arm, Stephanie Jean!"

"Oops." Stephanie held her hands in the air, feigning innocence.

"I'll wait till the weekend, *after* your birthday. In the meantime," she said, taking another cookie, "keep spoiling me."

The two women ate a half dozen cookies between them before finishing their tea and conversation for the evening. After a heartfelt hug, Stephanie retired, leaving Molly to lock up the house.

Stephanie placed the rest of her belongings in the dresser drawers, then slid the empty suitcases beneath the bed. Her gaze, like a magnet, was drawn to the drawer hiding Molly's peculiar treasures.

"I should've asked," she murmured as she opened the drawer. She took the slew of papers in her hand.

Returning to the bed, Stephanie fluffed the two pillows, turned on the headboard lamp, and lay down. She removed the first poem and set it beside her, focusing on the second page. A short poem, written in blue ink, was dated September 12, 1970.

> Lost, apart from birth to find
> the perfect match to fully bind
> And you I found to find you me,
> two together eternally.
>
> Longing hearts come together
> both in pieces, two by two.
> Half of yours and half of mine
> shall tightly mend the loving puzzle.
>
> Love,
> James

The writing struck Stephanie as beautiful, yet too intimate to read without permission. Still, her eyes fed on the words a second and third time.

Feeling ashamed, she climbed off the bed with the poems. She returned them to the drawer and shut it with finality, promising herself she would not open it again without Molly's approval.

CHAPTER TWO

Confession

Stephanie awoke the next morning at seven o'clock, but that was according to her own gold-plated watch, which she had not reset. She raised her head from her pillow and looked out the east window, finding the sun just rimming the top of Willow Mountain.

"It's only five," she muttered, letting her head fall back. She closed her eyes in a hasty attempt to return to sleep, but the sunrise-in-progress, alive and kicking in her mind's eye, beckoned. Giving in, Stephanie climbed out of bed and walked to the window. She drew open the curtains all the way.

"OK," she said toward the distant mountains and peekaboo sun, "show me your stuff." Then she watched one of the West's best shows.

After a glorious few minutes at the window, Stephanie headed for the bathroom, leaving the Lord to take care of turning the earth and lighting up Montana. She took a bubble bath in the cast iron, clawfoot tub beneath a large, clear plastic skylight, enjoying the brightening summer sky and feathered clouds drifting by as she lay back in the tub.

After drying off, she combed her shoulder-length hair and put on denim shorts and a forest green Eastern Michigan sweatshirt. She applied light makeup, then sat on the bed and slipped her feet into her sandals.

It's 7:40 in Michigan, she thought, *so Phil should be eating breakfast.* She picked up the telephone from the bedside table and dialed her husband.

"Hello, Kline residence."

Stephanie cooed and said, "This is your Montana cowgirl."

Phil chuckled. "Tell me more."

Charmingly, Stephanie recited, "Longing hearts come together, both in pieces, two by two. Half of yours and half of mine shall tightly mend the loving puzzle."

"Wow," Phil said. "Who wrote that?"

"What if I said I did?"

"You must've gotten bored on the plane, huh?"

"Some romantic you are!"

"Tough to be romantic when you're two thousand miles away and my cereal's getting soggy! But I love you just the same."

"I love you too," Stephanie said with a giggle. "Just called to say I miss you."

"I miss you too. How's Molly?"

"Great. She'll be forty-nine tomorrow, but doesn't look it. She's gorgeous."

"Like you?"

"You're sweet."

"I know," Phil kidded, "but Mister Sweet has to go to work."

"All right, I'll let you go, but I don't want to. Say hi to everyone at the bank."

"Before you hang up, who wrote—"

"The poem?" Stephanie blurted. "Molly's college sweetheart, James Wade."

"The guy killed in Vietnam?"

"Yes. Molly can't forget him."

"Hmm, too bad." Then with increased urgency, he said, "Steph, I've gotta go."

"OK, I love you. Be careful."

"You too. Love you."

Stephanie planted a kiss on the receiver's mouthpiece and hung up. She made her way to the kitchen, gathered up some eggs and bacon, and began fixing breakfast.

Molly entered the kitchen as Stephanie cracked the last of four eggs on the edge of a hot frying pan.

"Up kinda early, aren't you, Steph?"

Stephanie looked over her shoulder at Molly, who was at her disheveled worst in a ratty, red bathrobe. "Looks like you are too!"

"Not much choice when you're banging pans around like cymbals." Molly opened the bread box. "I'll burn the toast," she said, ignoring Stephanie's toothy grin. She dropped four slices of bread into the toaster. "I don't know where you get all this humor at six in the morning."

"Just like the good old days at EMU," Stephanie said with a chuckle. "You're still the same old early morning grump, more humorous than ever, and you don't even realize it!"

Molly had to laugh. "OK, I'll grin and bear it. Just make sure the bacon's real crispy."

"Like your toast?"

Molly shuffled out of the kitchen. "The bathroom beckons. Butter the toast. There's strawberry jam in the fridge and some orange juice in the freezer."

Stephanie let out a snort. "Like I've got ten hands, right?"

Molly disappeared without further comment, leaving Stephanie to the morning chores. Stephanie just shook her head, having accepted her friend's crack-of-dawn quirks a long time ago. She found the butter and jelly in the refrigerator, then opened the freezer to grab a small can of juice. She mixed the juice with water in a blender.

Of course, when the food was ready, Molly wasn't. Stephanie made a plate for herself and began eating. She had halfway finished before Molly entered the kitchen, still looking unruly, though a little more awake.

"You're a knockout," Stephanie remarked.

"My usual morning look," Molly said, shrugging. "No one to doll up for."

"Why not?"

Molly frowned. "Here we go again. Don't give me that how's-your-love-life routine, Steph."

"Why not?"

Molly sat down at the table and filled a plate. "This isn't my kind of breakfast talk." She picked up a piece of cold, buttered toast. "You pray?"

"For the food, for you, and your future boyfriend."

Molly bowed her head. "Dear Lord, may the subject be changed."

"OK," Stephanie said, waving her napkin in the air to surrender. "Tomorrow's your forty-ninth birthday."

"So now we'll discuss growing older and how fifty scares you. Another great topic."

"Fifty does scare me!" Stephanie said, laughing. "But what I wanted to talk about was shopping! What do you want for your birthday?"

Molly unceremoniously took a big bite of toast. With puffed cheeks, she said, "A good book would be fine."

"A food book?"

Molly covered her mouth with her hand, holding back a laugh and a lot of bread. She managed to swallow once before breaking up. "A *good* book, not a food book!"

Stephanie smiled. "Aren't they one in the same?"

Both women fell into a giggling fit, and Stephanie knew Molly's grouchiness had dissolved.

Three hours later, they were riding in Molly's newer car, a 1997 gray Volvo, having driven twenty-five of the forty miles to the mall in Missoula.

"Most of the shops open at nine," Molly reminded Stephanie, adjusting her sunglasses, "but the bookstore doesn't open till ten."

Nodding, Stephanie said, "I forgot the name of it."

"The Sequel. I could spend a paycheck in there." Molly took her eyes off the road and glanced at Stephanie. "You could, too, so remember: one book is enough. Don't buy me two or three."

Stephanie gazed at the jagged, forested mountains to the west and sighed. "Well, I guess this is as good a time as any."

"For what?"

"Remember last night when you told me to use your dresser?"

"Yes."

"Well, I opened a drawer to put some clothes away and I found—"

"My drawer of treasures!" Molly said with a chuckle.

"That's right!" Molly's laugh made Stephanie laugh, too, relieving her tension.

"What did you discover?" Molly asked. "Anything exciting?"

Stephanie looked at Molly's face, searching for a false front. "Well, I saw some sports tickets and old report cards and stuff."

Molly nodded her head. "Just little keepsakes," she affirmed.

"A stack of old poems too."

Molly eyed her old friend.

"I sort of accidentally-on-purpose read two of them."

Squeezing her eyes shut for a moment, Molly said, "James's poems."

"Yes," Stephanie whispered.

"I haven't read them in a while. They bring back too many memories . . . too many hopes and dreams . . ." Molly's voice cracked. "I kinda buried them in the drawer."

"I'm sorry I dug them out. I had no business—"

"Don't worry," Molly said, smiling frankly. "No harm done." She took off her sunglasses, set them on the dash, and rubbed her eyes. "I'm wondering, Steph . . ."

"About what?"

"Did you like the poems?"

Surprised by the question, Stephanie let out a laugh. "Like them? Yes, they were beautiful. That's why I read two of them."

Molly nodded. "Knowing you, it took all your willpower not to read more."

"I thought about nailing the drawer shut."

"Those poems are the most beautiful I've ever read," Molly said, giving her head a little shake. "We only had ten months together before James went to Vietnam."

"He and Bill Bayliss," Stephanie interjected.

"Best friends." Molly glanced at a car passing on her left. A pigtailed little girl in the rear seat with her nose pressed against the window waved, and Molly waved back.

"Anyway, James wrote me forty-nine poems over the next nine months." She looked at Stephanie wistfully. "I waited and waited for that fiftieth poem, but it never came. I've never fully recovered. With God's help, the pain has lessened over the years, but I still feel the loss."

Stephanie exhaled a long breath. "Have you seen James's dad since he moved to Florida?"

Molly shook her head. "I heard he remarried, but I haven't seen him since Mary died."

"What about Bill's family?"

"Nothing," Molly said.

"Oh." Stephanie slumped back in her seat. Suddenly, she bolted upright and pointed northwest toward a distant mountaintop. "Look, a fire!"

Molly studied the orange flames and plume of smoke. "That's a good five or six miles away, and it's not a controlled burn. It's a forest fire. Probably the first of the summer. We don't usually get fires until August."

"How do you know it's not a controlled burn?"

"First of all, it's too big," Molly observed, "and it's too widespread. Plus, there was some lightning last night, and that's usually how these fires get started."

"Are we supposed to call it in?"

"I'm sure the Forest Service is already on it. They've got lookout towers throughout the valley, so these fires are spotted right away. It's pretty routine."

"Routine? I wouldn't regard any fire as routine."

Molly laughed. "You don't think fire is fire is fire?"

"No," Stephanie said flatly. "Some are small and some are red-hot." She observed the fire on the mountain. "That one's red-hot."

"Kinda like, oh, your love for Phil?"

Stephanie's eyes popped wide open. "Red-hot?"

Molly stared at the road. "That's my point. That's why I haven't dated anyone since James. Our love was red-hot, and I won't just settle for an itty-bitty flame."

Stephanie bit her lip, deciding to let the conversation die. Then, in an instant, she changed her mind.

"How can you get a roaring fire going if you never light a match?"

"You don't understand, Steph. That fire over there is really gonna be something for a while, but when it gets put out, the whole mountainside will be damaged and scarred."

Stephanie nodded, waiting for more. She soon realized, however, that Molly was finished, leaving much unsaid.

"Maybe so, Moll, but just remember, next spring will bring new growth on that mountainside, and in a few years it'll make a comeback."

Molly, her jaw tightening, kept her eyes on the highway.

Stephanie sensed she had scored. She turned away, knowing it was time to be quiet.

CHAPTER THREE

Glimpses of Love and Life

The fire that Stephanie and Molly had seen southwest of the town of Lolo had grown to fifty acres and was getting some good attention. A type-two hand crew consisting of twenty firefighters had been deployed with Pulaskis (a tool that is half ax, half grub hoe) and combies (a combination tool that is fitted with a military-type trenching blade on one end and a pick on the other). Overhead, a Sikorsky Sky Crane was airborne.

On his initial run, the pilot hovered the helicopter several feet above the Bitterroot River, a few miles below the blaze, and pulled two thousand gallons of water through a hose and into the holding tanks in less than a minute. Then the Sky Crane lifted, skirted the trees, and ultimately delivered a curtain of water to the hottest part of the fire. Circling in a racetrack pattern, the pilot headed back to the river.

Thirty miles to the south, the knee-high flames of the Gash Peak fire roared through some tall grasses and snapped at brush and small trees. The Forest Service fire spotter at the Willow Mountain Lookout east of Corvallis had called the supervisor's office at the Hamilton Dispatch, and a fire crew from Stevensville Ranger Station was mobilized. At the same time, the humidity cratered to a mere 10 percent as southwesterly winds gusted to twenty-five miles an hour, adding up to a red flag warning for firefighters. With the weather change, the blaze worked itself into a frenzy in an area of downed timber, extending the flames a hundred feet into the air.

Molly parked her car in the Southgate Mall parking lot. She and Stephanie, both dressed in T-shirts and shorts, took their purses and walked in the invigorating morning sunshine to the mall entrance.

"We've got almost fifteen minutes till the bookstore opens," Molly said, entering the mall through a glass door. Stephanie followed behind her.

"So, let's shop!" Stephanie suggested. She gestured toward a sports store on her right. "I need a University of Montana sweatshirt for Phil."

"Every time you're here you buy him some Grizzlies stuff," Molly said, grinning. "He must get a kick out of it."

They walked into Universal Athletics.

"His friends are calling him Grizzly Phil," Stephanie said, "and the scary thing is, he seems to like it."

"Grizzly Phil? Not the greatest nickname for the vice-president of a bank."

Stephanie found a rack of sweatshirts. "He likes it on the golf course when he's chewing up the competition, like a hungry—"

"Grizzly bear!" chimed in Molly. They both laughed.

Fifteen minutes later, Stephanie toted a shopping bag with a Montana Grizzlies sweatshirt through the mall to the bookstore. Molly had ducked into another store, allowing Stephanie time to look for a birthday present.

"May I help you?" asked a handsome, bespectacled middle-aged salesman.

Stephanie looked into the man's smiling blue eyes. "Yes, um, are your books of poetry still in the back?"

"Right this way." The man headed toward the rear of the store, his long legs covering the distance quickly. Stephanie chuckled as she raced to keep up.

"Here we are!"

"Thanks, Tom," Stephanie said, reading his nametag. "Any new books you'd recommend?"

"As a matter of fact, there is this one, though it's expensive."

He pulled a tall, thin hardbound book from the shelf and handed it to her.

"*Glimpses of Love and Life* by Jonathan Roseland," Stephanie read from the cover.

"Do you like love poems?" Tom asked. He slid his round glasses higher on his sharply-cut nose.

Stephanie blushed. "Well, yes, but this book's for a friend."

A knowing grin spread across Tom's face. "If it's for Molly Meyers, you won't go wrong."

Stephanie's mouth fell open.

Shrugging, Tom said, "She comes here a lot."

"But how did you know I was—"

"I remember you from last summer. I saw you a couple times with Molly."

"Hmm." Uncomfortable with the situation, Stephanie tried to outmaneuver the clerk. "I'm sorry, but I don't remember you."

"That's OK. To be honest, it's Molly who I want to notice me."

"Molly?"

Tom nodded.

"Does she know it?"

"If she doesn't, something's definitely wrong with my technique," Tom replied. "I've asked her out three times."

Stephanie hiked her eyebrows. "Out? On a date?"

"Yes."

"And?"

"No go," Tom said, pushing a lock of curly brown hair up and away from his glasses. "She's nice to me, but she's turned me down every time."

Stephanie looked at the book in her hand. "That's life."

Tom laughed. "Yeah, that's life, all right. But I'll keep trying."

"Don't hold your breath," Stephanie warned.

"I won't." Tom turned to leave. "Let me know if you need any more help."

Stephanie watched Tom walk away. She decided he was OK, but figured he had no chance with Molly. *After all, what man did?*

She wedged her shopping bag under her arm, ran her fingers over the rose-colored dust jacket of the poetry book and lifted it to breathe in its aroma. She had loved the feel and smell of a new book ever since she was a little girl.

"The poem on page ten is nice," Tom called back.

Stephanie looked up as Tom disappeared into another aisle. She opened the book to page ten. The spine of the book was stiff, and Stephanie enjoyed hearing it crackle as she stretched out the cover. Her eyes fell on the poem, styled to appear handwritten.

SIMPLY, MY LOVE

My love is like a journey to the stars,
  like my pillow up in Mars.
My love is like a rainbow in the sky
  filled with colors, gets me high.
My love is like a rocket on the moon,
  like wedding bells in the middle of June.
My love is like a castle on a hill,
  like a whistling whippoorwill.
My love is like a butterfly in flight,
  like a missile out of sight.
My love is like the ocean's roar,
  like the mighty eagle's soar.
My love is like a singing lark,
  like a whitetail running in the park.
My love is like a field of rye,
  like a hummingbird in the sky.
My love is like a mountain tall,
  deeper than the waters fall.
My love is like the bluest streams,
  like the purest snow in my dreams.
My love . . .

That's pretty, Stephanie thought, admiring the accompanying photograph of an eagle with a mountain and rainbow in the background.

She leafed through several more pages, noting that a photograph complemented each of ninety-nine poems in the book. "No wonder it costs so much," she mused, pausing at a picture of a swallowtail butterfly floating over some sheet music on a patio table.

Stephanie read the poem on the opposite page.

MELODY

Bouncing in the sky,
Dotted eighth-notes on the breeze,
Are the butterflies.

"What a charming haiku!" Stephanie closed the book, deciding to purchase it.

Tom met her at the checkout counter. "I see you've taken my advice."

"Yes, it looks good."

"You won't regret it," he said, then added in the same breath, "and that'll be thirty-two dollars."

Stephanie took the cash from her purse. "At least there's no sales tax here. I'd pay almost two dollars more in Michigan."

"One of the many reasons I'm hooked on Montana," Tom said with a nice smile. He slipped the book into a plastic bag and took Stephanie's money.

"I'll let Molly know you found this for me."

"Thanks, I need all the help I can get."

Stephanie left the bookstore with her shopping bags in hand. Walking into the outer mall, she was pondering the encounter with Tom when Molly hailed her.

"You bought me a book!" Molly reached for the bag.

Stephanie shielded the gift from Molly's grasp. "How 'bout waiting till your birthday?"

"Come on, Steph, let me see it." They moved to a redwood bench next to a porcelain waterfall and sat down.

Stephanie set her purse and the sports bag at her feet. "I haven't written an inscription yet."

"Later," Molly suggested, snatching the book bag from Stephanie. Stephanie shrugged, so Molly went ahead and looked at her present.

"*Glimpses of Love and Life,*" she read aloud. "That sounds good." Then she read further, "A Book of Poetry by Jonathan Roseland."

She turned a few pages. "Dedicated to a long lost love—if only I could love a second time." Nodding, she replied, "I can relate to that."

Molly browsed through the book, reading a few of the poems and skimming others. She smiled at times, giving Stephanie the impression she was happy with the gift.

"I hope you like it," Stephanie said, anticipating a positive response.

Molly's grin suddenly vanished as her mouth gaped open.

"What's wrong?" Stephanie asked.

"I don't believe this!" Molly's eyes remained riveted to the page.

"What?"

"Look at this poem." Molly handed the book to Stephanie, who read the poem.

FOR KEEPS

Running on the beach
all day with you,
throwing sand in the wind
and kicking a blue-and-white ball
against the rocks,
yelling and laughing
and stomping down deserted

little sand castles,
finally stopping
to lie down and sleep.

I awake,
finding you have buried me
to the neck in mud
so you can kiss and keep me
forever.

Stephanie gazed at Molly. "What about it?"
Trembling, Molly said, "That was written by James!"
"You're kidding! You sure?"
"I've read that poem a thousand times."
"No way!"
"I'm telling you, that's James's poem!"
Stephanie gave the book back to Molly. "See if you recognize
any others."
Molly hurried through the pages, mumbling to herself.
"Someone's playing a trick on me."
Suddenly she froze.
"What?"
Molly tapped her finger on a page. "Here's another one!"
Stephanie looked at the poem.

TO MY LOVE, SOMEWHERE

You're enchanting and beautiful
and I love your poetry.
That is all I want to tell you
but I can't seem to find you
in crowds or alone.
You're exquisite in my memory
on sidewalks
in classrooms
writing poetry on blackboards,

reciting poems in the shade,
but I can't seem to find you.
I only hear your name
on the wind
in the mangroves
where rivers float my sorrows
and gush of things lost.

"James wrote that?"

Bewildered, Molly burst into tears. Stephanie embraced her.

The women remained, one friend holding the other, for what seemed like forever to Stephanie. A hundred thoughts went through her mind.

What do we do? Who is Jonathan Roseland? Did he plagarize James's poems? How? Whom do we call? What do I say?

"Let's pull ourselves together and figure this out," Stephanie whispered in Molly's ear.

Molly wiped her eyes. Looking at Stephanie, she said, "James must somehow . . . he must be alive!"

Stephanie swallowed hard, her arms going numb. She had hoped Molly would not fly to that crazy conclusion.

Chapter Four

The Poet

The poet sat at his desk in the small living room, ignoring the blank piece of paper he had inserted in the typewriter moments earlier. His eyes focused instead on the whitetail doe just outside his picture window. He recognized her immediately as the one he called No Fear. An odd dark patch above her right eye gave away her identity.

She stopped walking—perhaps oblivious of his attention, perhaps not—and stared into the glass. She changed the tilt of her head once, then again, keeping her gaze.

Maybe she's seeing herself for the first time, he thought. Surely there had been reflections observed at watering holes, but this was a fine chance for detail.

After a minute, the doe turned and slowly moved off.

The poet returned to his work, eyeing the paper that reflected nothing, not the slightest thought. His mind seemed just as blank.

He decided to close his eyes, and there he saw the deer. She was his message, his inspiration. *No Fear.* He smiled.

In a rush, his fingers danced on the keys. He wrote. He composed. To him, a symphony.

BOW HUNT

Crouched in an hour-old blind,
eyeing night away,
holding razored death at a near draw.
Cold steeled muscles throb,
painfully coiled,
strained to their tearing point.
Spineless winds knife the back,
whipping bared cheeks,

beating against the threatening, untried heart.
The last colored leaves wrestle to free themselves,
violently rattling their loosening chains.
Hopelessly,
dying shadows surrender
to morning's birth of light.
Eyes, deadly,
scan the forest,
searching for running blood.
The first shriek of exposed life
shakes the steady, awakens the silent.
Adrenalin surges, a stick cracks,
and the eyes find red
standing nervously aware,
quivering,
fearfully indecisive.
Cramped muscles spring,
death rips the air
and exploding deer vanish
into the mist.

The poet, on the edge of his chair after striking the final key, hung there. He was in a familiar place, somewhere between reservation and fulfillment. He leaned toward the latter, keenly reading his composition.

"Almost," he whispered before dropping his arms and relaxing. He exhaled, tossed his head back, and emotionally disconnected from his writing.

A minute later he reached for the black wooden cane that stood against the desk. Climbing clumsily to his feet, he wielded the cane at his left side and limped down the hallway toward the bathroom. He exaggerated the limp as he went, testing the muscles in his reconstructed left hip. Just short of the bathroom door, he paused in front of the framed photograph of a beautiful young woman, then shook his head and moved on.

As he approached the mirror above the bathroom sink, he remembered No Fear at his window. *She had been eager to see herself,* he thought, the idea in sharp contrast to his own rising apprehension. He had no desire, but he had to look.

He leaned his six-foot frame over the sink and stared into his own hazel eyes reflected in the mirror, depressed by the sight. His left eye drooped grotesquely, tearing up, as usual. He had no eyelashes.

He looked at his bald, scarred head, then to the brown wig on the counter. After hooking his cane on the towel rack, he took the hairpiece and fit it in place. Then he plucked an artificial ear from its plastic case, turning slightly until the steel knob on the left side of his head became visible in the mirror. He attached the prosthesis before mussing some hair to partially conceal it.

Finished with the essentials, he attempted a smile. His cheeks lifted but the synthetic lips would not curl. He knew they couldn't; still he had checked them a hundred thousand times.

"A dreamer whose dreams are dead," he said, summarizing his existence, as far as he was concerned, in a single utterance. The words, pronounced with a slight lisp, sounded hollow in his good right ear. But they rang brutally true in his heart.

He turned from the mirror, grabbing his cane, and made his way back to his desk chair.

"Come back, No Fear," he spoke at the window through which he viewed birch trees and, further out, a broken-down wooden fence. A red squirrel sat hunched on one of the fence posts, but at thirty yards he couldn't make out which squirrel—Chummy or Edgy. The fur on Chummy's back was the redder of the two; otherwise, the rodents seemed identical. Up close, however, their personalities were enough for the poet to distinguish between them—Chummy was chummy, almost eating out of his hand, while Edgy would not come within twenty feet without a serious nervous twitch.

The poet wondered where Kelly, his twelve-year-old Irish setter, had gone since he had let her out the door more than an hour ago. Her time outside rarely lasted more than ten or fifteen minutes before she'd scratch at the door wanting in. She was no longer the tireless runner of her youth, having become a sleepy house dog.

She's off somewhere, he thought, *or the deer and the squirrel wouldn't have come.*

Just then the phone on the desk rang. He scooted his chair forward and grabbed the receiver, bringing it to his good ear.

"Hello?" he said.

"Jonathan, this is Eric Maclellan."

The poet sat back. "Hi, Eric. How are you?"

"I've got good news about your book. It's selling well, even better than we'd hoped."

The poet hesitated, not ready to embrace the report. Forcing himself, he said, "Great, I'm glad."

Eric laughed. "Well, I hope so. I've got a few book signings I'm lining up and a TV interview. The first signing is right there in Coeur d'Alene at Woody's Books, a week from tomorrow. I know it's short notice, but everything's set, OK?"

The poet's breath caught in his throat.

"Jonathan? You there?"

"Uh, yes. I'm surprised, that's all. Can I call you back?"

"Is something wrong?"

Something wrong? How about my wrecked face? He remembered the single photograph he had sent Maclellan showing himself sitting on his porch with his face turned away, half hidden with a hand on his chin. Even his brown wig was shrouded by a black felt cowboy hat with the brim pulled down.

After taking a deep breath, the poet said, "Um, I don't look so good, not for television."

Eric chuckled. "You mean you're not as handsome as I might've imagined? So what? They have makeup artists to spruce you up."

"It's not that easy. What about my lisp?"

"Oh, don't worry, Jonathan. It's not even noticeable. You'll be fine. I'll set everything up and get back with you." Eric paused for a reaction, but when none was offered, he said good-bye.

The poet mumbled something, then heard the click in his ear. He sat frozen, staring into space. A new nightmare had begun.

CHAPTER FIVE

Questions

Molly lifted the book from her lap. Turning to the back cover, she found what she wanted.

"Listen to this," she told Stephanie. "'Jonathan Roseland resides in Idaho, where he writes poetry and takes care of his devoted Irish setter.'" She silently read the words a second time. "It doesn't say he's married."

Stephanie shook her head. "That doesn't mean it's James."

Molly grabbed her purse from the bench and prepared to move. "How did you ever choose this book, Steph?"

"Um, I liked the poetry and . . . um, Tom . . ."

"Tom Hathaway?" Molly rose to her feet.

Stephanie gathered her shopping bag and purse and stood up. "The clerk?"

Molly scowled. "How could he?" She marched off toward the bookstore.

Stephanie caught Molly's arm. "Wait a minute! There's no way he could've had anything to do with this!"

Molly pulled her arm free and resumed her walk, albeit with less steam. Stephanie noted that the closer they got to the store's entrance, the slower the pace became.

She's thinking things through, Stephanie figured.

By the time the women approached Tom Hathaway, who was inspecting a magazine rack, Molly had pulled herself together.

"Tom," she said in a normal tone of voice.

He turned around and broke into a warm smile. "Hi, Molly."

She held up the book, saying nothing.

"Is something the matter?" Tom asked.

Molly gave the book a little shake. "Do you know anything about this or the author?"

Tom shrugged. "Not much. Only that it's new and really popular." He glanced at Stephanie, looking for help.

She offered some. "Tom, that book contains some poems that belong to Molly . . ."

Tom's eyes grew bigger.

". . . so we need to know more about this Jonathan Roseland. Has he published any other books?"

"I don't think so," Tom replied, looking at Molly, "but we can find out." He started for the front of the store, motioning for the women to follow.

Over his shoulder, Tom said, "I'll look him up on the computer. The publisher is Fawnhaven, right?"

Molly looked at the spine of the book. "That's right."

"They're in Portland." Tom stepped behind the counter where the computer sat. The women stood by as Tom began his search.

"Let's see," he mumbled, typing quickly.

Stephanie glanced at Molly, whose eyes were glued to Tom's every move. Stephanie was dreading the implausible mess she and Molly were falling into. She visualized spending the next nine days of her vacation chasing after a ghost. Then she felt selfish for having had such a thought.

"Here we are," Tom said, studying the computer screen. "*Glimpses of Love and Life,* copyright 1999. I believe that's his only book."

Molly looked at Stephanie. "Now what?"

"Um, we need an address. Jonathan Roseland's address."

"The only way to get his address is by calling the publisher," Tom stated, "and I'm sure they won't give it out."

Molly opened the front cover of the poetry book and flipped a page. "Fawnhaven Publishers, Inc.," she said. "Portland, Oregon. No street address. No phone number."

"Don't worry, I can pull up that information on the computer,"

Tom said. He glanced at his wristwatch. "It's 9:30 there, so I'll call them."

Molly's nerves, usually steady, had come undone. Her breathing was shallow. Myriads of questions spawned in her brain, entangling in midthought. She lost her place, awash in a dream, then it all flushed in a downward spin.

"Molly!" Stephanie broke Molly's faint halfway to the floor. Purses and shopping bags and the poetry book tumbled about them.

"Oh!" Molly said from her knees. "What?" She blinked rapidly, wondering about the commotion.

Tom helped her to get up. Stephanie scooped up the spillage while Tom ushered Molly to a reading area where a sofa and two upholstered chairs had been placed.

"I'm fine," Molly insisted.

"Sit here and relax," Tom said.

Stephanie hurried to catch up before dumping her possessions in a chair. She sat down on the couch and dragged Molly with her.

"I'll be right back," Tom said.

Molly lay her head back and gazed at the ceiling. She drew a long breath. "Sorry for going bananas, Steph."

"That's OK, Moll, I understand. We've been thrown a curve."

"I'll get it together," Molly said. "The last thing I want is to ruin your vacation. I'm sorry."

Stephanie took Molly's hand. "You've done nothing wrong."

Molly frowned. "Someone has."

Stephanie thought about it. "Yes, someone's done somebody wrong."

"You're looking at the somebody," Molly declared.

When Tom returned, he was carrying a note card.

"What happened?" Molly asked.

"I finally got through to an editor named—" he looked at the card—"Eric Maclellan. He said he couldn't give me a writer's personal information."

Tom gave the card to Molly.

"Didn't you tell him about my poems?"

"Well, I told him Roseland's book contained some of your poems, but that's all I knew."

Stephanie put her face in her hand. "Great," she mumbled.

"But," Tom rallied, "the little I said got his attention. There's his phone number, a direct line to his office. He wants you to call back."

Molly stared at the card in her hand and watched it shake. "Call back?"

"Yes, he said if there's anything to this, call him back."

Molly looked to Stephanie.

Seeing fear in her friend's eyes, Stephanie got up and grabbed her things from the chair. She handed Molly her purse and the poetry book.

"Come on, let's go home."

CHAPTER SIX

Bad Times

The crew boss at Stevensville Ranger Station had momentary trouble rounding up a second team of firefighters. Meanwhile, the Gash Peak blaze had made a run down the northeast face of the mountain toward tiny Glen Lake, engulfing three hundred acres in less than an hour. A slurry bomber with a load of fire retardant had been flown over the leading edge of the fire, but the ensuing drop proved ineffective as strong winds simply carried sparks over the orange-colored swath; hence, the fire "jumped" the line.

The residents in and around Victor began spreading the word about the enormous cloud of smoke to the northwest of town. Several vehicles had been seen traveling up rugged Glen Lake Trailhead Road in the direction of the fire, transporting gawkers and camera buffs who wanted a close-up look before police or Forest Service personnel could close the road. But most people carried on with their daily routines, periodically casting anxious eyes toward the billowing smoke.

The poet climbed into his truck after Kelly, laid his cane between himself and the dog, and started the engine. He glanced at his face in the rearview mirror, yanked the brim of his straw cowboy hat lower, and backed out of his driveway.

Coeur d'Alene, Idaho, with its majestic mountains and beautiful lake, was ten minutes away. It was a town the poet loved but seldom enjoyed, staying away to avoid the stares and whispers. Biweekly trips to a small grocery store called Wayne's Market were a necessity, however; and to Wayne Summers, the fiftyish pot-bellied proprietor, the poet was just another customer. In fact,

Wayne knew the poet only as "Jon" and wasn't even aware of his book, though he had attempted on several occasions to strike up a friendly conversation.

As the poet drove his truck, his thoughts weren't on his grocery list, let alone the wonderful scenery. He was tormented by the sudden demand for personal appearances while knowing he couldn't possibly come before the public. Never in his wildest dreams had he envisioned his poetry being published in the first place. He had never before sought recognition; in his mind, his real self was beyond recognition in any way. But on a whim, in a wild shot at securing a smidgen of self-worth and perhaps a reason for his existence, he had mailed a hundred and fifty poems to Fawnhaven Publishers, bracing himself for the rejection he believed would follow. Rejection, after all, had long ago become a familiar thorn.

A phone call from Eric Maclellan changed everything, albeit not right away. Initially, Maclellan admitted that publishing a book of poetry was a modest enterprise but one Fawnhaven had chosen to pursue. He offered a standard contract with a five-thousand-dollar advance.

The poet, apprehensive and suddenly rethinking his situation, declined Maclellan's proposal. But when the editor tripled the advance, the poet's poor financial status dictated his acceptance. He took the money and shrank back into reclusiveness for a year, generally dreading the book's release, yet strangely hopeful at times. Occasionally, he dared to speculate that something good would come of this, something to connect him to the living, even if from a distance. He imagined his words touching hearts and moving people emotionally in a manner totally opposite to the way his physical presence moved them.

"We're here," he told his dog, parking in front of the market. Kelly already knew where they were, and she knew her place was to wait for her master. She watched him dab the water from his left eye, adjust the collar on his Polo shirt, take his cane, and slide his lanky body out of the truck.

The poet's first steps toward the store's entrance were interrupted by a small towheaded boy on a skateboard who abruptly stopped short of colliding with him. When their eyes met, the boy grinned momentarily before looking scared.

The poet smiled. "You look like an expert," he said, hoping for acceptance.

The boy glanced behind him, checking his escape route.

"I was really good on a skateboard once," the poet said, but the boy quickly grabbed his board and turned to run.

In a flash, he was gone.

The poet looked back at Kelly. She sat bolt upright at the half-open passenger window, her big brown eyes gazing at him.

At least Kelly loves me. "Good girl," he called to her before entering the store.

"Hello, Jon." Wayne Summers, wearing a white butcher's apron, was working the checkout counter.

"Good morning," the poet responded as he secured a grocery cart. He hooked his cane on the handle and pushed the cart into the first aisle. There he picked up a bag of apples and was busy selecting a grapefruit when someone came up behind him.

"Hey, you!"

The poet partially turned toward a stout, angry-looking man with big clenched fists.

"Why'd you scare my kid?" the man demanded. As the poet squarely faced him, the man suddenly went pale. He dropped his hands and sank a few inches. "Oh . . . I'm sorry. I, uh, I know you didn't mean nothin'."

The man spun around and hurried away.

Some predicament, the poet mused. *I handled the whole thing without speaking a word.*

Shaking his head, he returned to his shopping, filling his cart with cereals, canned goods, dog food, and other essentials. All the while, his mind was in a fog.

Halfway down the last aisle, he felt lightheaded and his vision suddenly blurred. He knew what was coming; it had happened a thousand times before.

Clutching his cart with both hands in an effort to steady himself, the flashback hit. That unforgettable moment in the Rung Sat Special Zone roared through him like an F-5 tornado. He saw Bill Bayliss firing an M-60 machine gun at an enemy hootch as he himself ran and jumped into a canal—plowing through water and up the bank—firing his M-79 grenade launcher at the door of the hootch—a 40mm grenade detonating, collapsing the thatched roof and walls and revealing a bunker—gunfire erupting like hard-driving rain—Bayliss screaming and stumbling—"I'm hit bad!"—the white phosphorus grenade exploding on his own web belt—falling into water, his body on fire—burning, burning, burning—unquenchable fire—"He shoulda died"—"No one can live like that"—"He'd be better off dead"—"God help him."

As the scene faded, the poet found himself sitting on the floor next to his shopping cart, soaked with perspiration. He held a zucchini in his hands as though it were a rifle. Wayne Summers was crouched beside him while two elderly women stood back in alarm.

"You OK, Jon?" Wayne asked twice.

The poet handed the zucchini to the grocer. "I'm sorry," he muttered, wiping saliva from his mouth and his blue jeans. "Please help me up."

Wayne pulled him to his feet.

Grasping his cart's handle, the poet said, "I . . . I'd better go." He began walking the cart toward the front of the store.

"You sure you're all right?" Wayne asked, moving alongside his customer.

"Just some bad memories, that's all."

"Vietnam?"

The poet nodded his head.

"I was there, too, with Bravo Platoon on the USS *Jennings County*," Wayne said.

"You were a Navy SEAL?" the poet asked, stopping at the checkout counter. "I was at Nha Be with Foxtrot Platoon."

"No kidding!" Wayne stepped behind the cash register. "Where were you when you got hit?"

Setting a soup can on the counter, the poet decided he was talking too much. Wayne Summers, however, was of the opposite bent, happy to discover a fellow warrior. He noted the poet's sudden silence, though, and opted to tread lightly.

"Anytime you'd like to get together, Jon, let me know," Wayne said, smiling. He rang up the groceries and bagged them himself.

The poet paid in cash, then wheeled the cart out of the store. Wayne watched him go, hopeful that a friendship would develop over time.

I don't even know his last name, Wayne thought, *but his scars on the outside aren't half as bad as on the inside. Of that, I'm sure.*

CHAPTER SEVEN

Getting Worse

When the poet got home, Chummy and Edgy darted across the driveway and up the trunk of a birch tree. The squirrels climbed higher as the truck stopped and Kelly jumped out and loped in their direction.

"Don't scare away our only friends, Kelly!" the poet said with a touch of sarcasm. He carried a bag of groceries to his house, thinking about how badly his day had been going. *It can't get much worse.*

He left the bag on the front porch and returned to the truck twice more for the others. As he reached the porch for the last time, he heard the telephone ringing.

"Let it ring," he said, opening the door. He bypassed the phone on his desk and walked to the kitchen counter, where he set the heaviest grocery bag and deposited his hat. Removing a half gallon of milk, he put it in the refrigerator. The phone continued to ring.

Annoyed, the poet walked to the living room and snatched up the receiver. He put it to his ear without speaking.

"Hello, Jonathan?"

With a sigh, the poet said, "Hello, Eric."

"Yes, it's me again! I've been calling for twenty minutes, but—"

"I was out shopping."

"Getting new clothes for your book signings?" Eric asked with a chuckle.

"Something like that," came the dry reply.

"Well, Jon, listen. I've got a bit of a problem, and you're the only one who can solve it." Maclellan's tone became so serious that the poet's stomach turned. "It's pretty strange."

The poet drew the chair out from his desk and sat down. "What is it?"

"I got a call from a woman in Victor, Montana. Her name is. . . let's see . . . I've got it right here. Molly Meyers."

Maclellan kept talking, but the poet's focus went haywire. He stared blankly out the window, cognizant of a red dog in the act of barking at a red squirrel in surrealistic slow motion. The yap seemed long in coming to his ear, and when it slapped, it was followed by a mind-numbing buzz.

Dropping the phone, he put his face in his hands. He closed his eyes only to see a girl running in a wheat field, laughing and joyful. She was Molly Meyers, with wind-blown hair and a beauty to die for.

> O, girl with the honey voice,
>   speak to me, my dear.
> Your loving words make me weak
>   when they kiss my ear.
> I miss you more than madly,
>   I long to touch your face.
> The thought of coming close to you
>   causes blood to race.
> Though miles separate our souls,
>   you're here within my heart.
> Our hands are destined to be joined,
>   clutching for a start.
> O, hold me in your dreams, my dear,
>   girl with the honey voice.
> Soon I'll gaze into your eyes,
>   rejoice! rejoice! rejoice!

". . . still there, Jonathan? Hello, Jonathan?"

The poet shook his head, then fumbled for the telephone. "Yes, I'm here. I just . . . the phone slipped out of my hand."

"Did you hear what I said about your poems? About this lady saying they belonged to her and a guy named James something?"

Composing himself, the poet took a breath. "Don't worry, Eric, the poems are all mine." He paused to wipe his eye, then added, "I can fix everything with one phone call to . . . Molly." Just saying her name pricked his conscience. He also knew he had misspoken, for the phone call that might "fix everything" for Fawnhaven would surely blow up his own life a second time, not to mention Molly's.

"You know her, then?"

"I used to. It's a long story."

"Were you married or something?"

"No, no . . . do you have her phone number?"

Maclellan gave it to him. "So, I don't have to be concerned about this, then?"

"You don't," the poet replied. "I'll take it from here." He said good-bye and hung up, wondering how and when he would "take it from here."

"This wasn't supposed to happen," he mumbled, falling back in his chair. What were the chances of Molly reading his book—and particularly the three poems he had written for her so many years ago? And why, for heaven's sake, did he allow those three to be included in the first place?

Living a lie had been hard. Assuming a false identity had been painful. Jonathan was a name he more or less had randomly chosen. Roseland was the name of the cemetery where Bill Bayliss's body had been buried. James Wade had been dead now for almost three decades to all but his parents, who themselves hadn't even known the truth for the first six months. Then they had been sworn to secrecy, agreeing only because they believed that James would show himself to everyone else within a short time. But as James first experimented with revealing himself to strangers, the horrific reactions he received toward his physical deformities drove him into a shell. A short time became a few years, then longer. James Wade, he ultimately resolved, could never be resurrected, especially to Molly.

"Molly," he said softly, looking at the phone number he had copied. The 406 area code surprised him, and as he folded the paper and slipped it into his wallet, he wondered if Molly were truly a Montana resident. Many years earlier he had quit torturing himself with checking up on her life in Michigan. He let go of her. The severance seemed to squash the little life left in him, and over the next year or two he accepted the self-proclaimed status of a walking dead man with nothing to live for. Barely existing, he carried on, periodically contacting his parents. He loved Chuck and Mary but had moved far away from them, unable to endure their constant pleadings for him to end his "pity party" as they called it.

Then, five years ago, Mary died. The poet sent flowers and called his father the day before the funeral, asking forgiveness for not attending, still avoiding exposure. But Chuck told his son if he didn't show up there would be no further communication between them. Then he hung up on his son's woeful life.

What a mess, the poet thought. *I've spared so many by my isolation, and now I'm forced to blast out of the dark like a chain saw. The first words from my mouth will cut Molly in two.*

CHAPTER EIGHT

Pins and Needles

Molly and Stephanie saw the column of smoke when they were still fifteen miles from Molly's house.

"Another fire!" Stephanie exclaimed.

"Yes," said Molly, shifting her gaze from the smoke to the road as she drove the car.

"Routine?"

Molly gulped. "Don't think so."

"I hope it's not your house, Moll."

"Looks like ten houses," Molly asserted, stepping on the gas.

Several minutes later, Molly knew that the fire was far from her home, which relieved her. But a few minutes after that, she stopped beside a police car that was parked a quarter mile from her driveway on White's Lane.

Cliff Casman, a hulking deputy sheriff whom Molly knew from church, leaned out his driver's side window. "Hi, Molly," he said with a friendly grin. His squinty eyes were swallowed up by his chunky, round face.

"How bad is the fire?" Molly asked, leaving her car idling.

"It's growin' fast, but it's still five miles from here. You can go home, but I'm here to give you and your neighbors notice of a possible threat to your property."

"Meaning what, exactly?"

"The next couple days will tell the story," Cliff replied, still smiling. "If this thing keeps comin', we'll be in a Stage 1/Alert. If that happens, I'll personally knock on your door and tell you."

"A Stage 1/Alert?"

Cliff nodded. "That means you'll be advised of the emergency, and we'll have a recommended response. Stage 2's a warnin' of the probability for evacuation."

"There's a Stage 3, I presume?" Molly pressed forward.

"Stage 3's a request for occupants of the affected area, which is the White's Lane and Iroquois Trail neighborhoods, to leave within a certain time frame and to check in at an evacuation center. Stage 4 is mandatory evacuation."

"Gee, Cliff, could all this happen?"

Shrugging, Cliff said, "It's too early to tell. There're firefighters on their way up there right now." He stuck a toothpick in the corner of his mouth. "If I were you, I wouldn't be too worried, though. From what I'm told, the fire's two miles southwest of Glen Lake. To reach your house, it'd have to go 'round the lake, burn due west for two miles to Smith Creek Drainage, then come a mile down the drainage to your backyard. That won't happen in a day, Molly."

"So, what should I do?" Molly wondered.

"Oh, just box up a few things. Put your important papers, family pictures, and keepsakes in a corner of your front room so you can get 'em out easy. That's all for now, I'd say."

Molly looked at the dome of smoke, then at Stephanie. "Having fun yet?"

Stephanie smirked. "Lots."

"Thanks, Cliff," Molly said, turning back toward the deputy. "Don't leave me hanging."

"You'll hear from me again if and when we reach Stage 1," the officer assured her.

Molly put her car in gear and drove away.

Molly sat at her kitchen table while Stephanie made coffee. The book of poetry lay open on the table, and Molly stared at a poem.

FIRST LOVE

I remember my first date.
I was thirteen
and a baseball star.
A girl from Arizona
fell for my pitching
on summer vacation
and I fell for her
because she could catch
a curve ball.
I took her
to a major league game
really thinking
she was the greatest,
but by the third inning
I had traded her
for Yogi Berra.

"I wonder if that editor believed a word I said," Molly mused. She flipped the book's cover shut.

"I'm sure he'll check it out," Stephanie replied. "All he has to do is call the author."

"And what if he lies? What if—"

"Then we'll find Jonathan Roseland and confront him ourselves," Stephanie said, pouring a cup of coffee at the kitchen counter. "We're lucky he lives right next door."

"Right next door?"

"Idaho!" Stephanie smiled as she set the coffee cup on a napkin in front of Molly.

Molly scowled. "Very funny."

"I'm not trying to be funny," Stephanie said, returning to the counter for her own cup. "Now that I've had time to think about it, I think it's more than coincidence that he lives so close, say, closer than Texas. I think God's hand is in this, and I know we can find this guy. We're within striking distance."

"Sorry this had to happen now. Plus there's a fire to worry about."

Stephanie sat down across from Molly. "Actually, the timing is probably perfect. You need me to be here."

Molly nodded her head, then both women sipped their coffee.

"Steph, what if it's James?" Molly asked.

"How could it be? We went to his funeral back in 1971."

"But that was a memorial service! There was no body!"

Shrugging, Stephanie said tersely, "How could he be alive and not contact you for twenty-eight years, Moll?"

Molly covered her face with her hands. "I don't know . . . I just don't know."

Stephanie stood up. She walked around the table, intending to give Molly a hug, but the phone rang.

Molly gave Stephanie a wide-eyed look.

"I'll get it," Stephanie said. She picked up the kitchen wall phone. "Hello."

Molly watched Stephanie's face for any telltale signs.

"She really can't talk right now," Stephanie spoke into the receiver, "but she's doing all right." She winked at Molly. "You heard about the fire? No, it's west of town. It's not a threat to any homes yet."

"Who is it?" Molly whispered.

"No, nothing yet," Stephanie replied, ignoring Molly's gesturings. "We talked to the editor, and we're waiting for him to call back."

After a pause, she said, "OK, Tom, thanks for calling." Then she hung up the phone.

"Tom Hathaway?"

"Yes, just wondering about the fire and how everything else is turning out." Stephanie sat down and took a drink of her coffee.

"Yeah, well, I'm wondering the same thing," Molly groused, "and every minute's like an hour."

"Have patience," Stephanie said.

"Patience. I know all about patience. It's been a yoke around my neck for so long, I think it's worn through. I'm on pins and needles."

"You'll be all right."

"What makes you think so?"

"Well, Moll, if Jonathan Roseland isn't James, then you'll just keep on living like you've been."

"Yeah," Molly gnarled, "as long as there's a good explanation concerning my poems!"

Stephanie nodded. "Understood. Now, if by some miracle James is alive, well . . ."

"Well, what?"

Stephanie sipped her coffee, eyeing Molly. She was suddenly overwhelmed by love and compassion for her friend.

"You've got tears in your eyes," Molly said.

Stephanie laughed, putting down her cup. "Don't you think I know it?"

"Why are you crying?"

Wiping her eyes, Stephanie contemplated an answer. Mostly, she knew, she was feeling sorry for Molly, but that part she would keep to herself. "I just, well, I love you, that's all," she said, snatching a napkin from the table and immodestly blowing her nose.

"You can only blow like that in front of people who love you back," Molly said, making Stephanie giggle.

Molly squinted her eyes, turning serious again. "So, tell me, best buddy, what if James is alive? How do I handle it?"

Stephanie squinted back. "Listen, Moll. The hardest thing you ever did was handle James's death. Handling this has gotta be easier."

"But it involves a big lie."

"Yeah, but that's easier than dealing with a death."

Unyielding in her stare, Molly grumbled, "Maybe; maybe not."

Stephanie blinked, then looked away, deciding to end the deadlock.

"I hope he's alive," Molly said, unwilling to change the subject. "I pray he is. I want the chance to deal with it. But he can't be, can he?" She rolled her eyes. "Can you believe we're having this conversation?"

"No," Stephanie said. "After all these years, I don't know what to say. This is nuts. It's inconceivable."

Molly slumped in her chair. "This is all so weird. Right out of left field."

CHAPTER NINE

Mingled Emotions

The call from left field came a couple hours later. Molly and Stephanie were busy sorting through some of Molly's legal papers in the kitchen after a midafternoon lunch. Molly looked at Stephanie when the phone rang and raised her eyebrows, signal enough for Stephanie.

Picking up the phone, Stephanie said hello. No one responded, so she said it again.

"Yes," a strange voice answered, "is Molly Meyers there?"

A shiver ran through Stephanie's body. She glanced at Molly, who was all eyes, afraid to hand her the phone. She decided to get more from the caller.

"May I ask who this is?"

There was a long pause. Stephanie's heart beat faster as she asked again.

"Is this, um, Stephanie?" the voice came back.

Stephanie swallowed hard. Her tongue felt stuck to the roof of her mouth. She pried it loose and managed one word. "James?"

Molly watched Stephanie's face, and as the expression turned aghast, she stepped forward and seized the phone.

"James?" she demanded.

"Molly?"

Molly knew the voice, and the sound of it sent an electric jolt through her that crumpled her knees. She stumbled to a chair, stifling a shriek.

"Molly?" resounded in her ear.

With the room spinning, Molly stretched the phone cord, sat

down, and shut her eyes. Fighting hyperventilation, she gulped a short breath, then whispered, "James. It's really you?"

"It's me," he said, then both of them broke down and wept.

Between sobs, James choked, "I'm sorry, Molly."

"You're alive!" she cried, looking toward Stephanie but seeing only a blur. Her breathing was hurried. "How can it be?"

"I'm not . . . not really alive."

"What do you mean?"

He tried to catch his breath, then sputtered and coughed. Collecting himself, he said, "The man you knew was . . . was killed in Vietnam."

Molly's arms went numb. *Help me, God!* "The man I knew? What are you saying?"

He hesitated, searching for the right words. "I, ah . . . I was wounded . . . burned, badly. Nobody knew who I was for six weeks, not even me." He listened for a moment to Molly's erratic breathing. "They didn't even try to save me. Then when I wouldn't die, or couldn't, I needed twenty operations just to . . . to look human again."

The phone shook against Molly's head. She grasped it with both hands. "But . . . but now you're OK, right?"

James tried to answer, but the words stuck in his throat. He could only sob.

"James!" Molly pleaded. Her whole body quaked.

"I'm sorry. I'm a mess, can't you tell?"

Molly forced a deep breath, fighting to get a grip. She doubled up her left fist and rapped it against her forehead. "You? You're a mess? What about me? You never should've abandoned me!"

"You don't understand," he responded defensively. "I wanted to protect you."

"Protect me? From what? Your death?" Her chin fell to her chest, and she let out a plaintive cry. "It didn't work, James, it didn't work. I've faced your death ten thousand times—unprotected—every day of my life."

Her words hit like a boxer's uppercut, making him sick to his stomach. Everything he had done, everything he had believed and all of his reasonings, were now on the line.

"Please listen," he begged. "I loved you so much, Molly, and you deserved the best. After Vietnam, I couldn't give you anything but the worst. There was nothing to give but a shattered, hideous life. An awful life."

"Who said so?" Molly asked, drooping in her chair. "You made the choice, and I had no say at all. Right?"

"I . . . well, yes, that's . . . that's right."

"What about your heart?"

"My heart?"

"Yes."

"What do you . . . mean?"

"Was your heart wounded?"

James knew he was had. "No," he said softly.

Choking back the tears, Molly uttered, "Then why in God's name did you destroy mine?"

James cringed. "You don't understand. You'd have to see me to understand."

"Well, I want to understand," Molly said, sensing a dash of hope. She sat up. "I've got to see you."

"I . . . I can't."

"You owe it to me, James!"

"Please, no."

"Yes," Molly demanded, "it'll happen. It's got to happen. Tell me where we can meet."

James uttered a weak "No."

"Don't make me struggle to find you," Molly implored. She wiped her tears on the back of her hand. "I've gone through enough. More than enough. You live in Idaho. Where?"

Begrudgingly, James replied, "Coeur d'Alene."

"I've been there!" Molly exclaimed. "I can't believe you live there. I'm just four hours away!"

"I don't think it's a good idea for us—"

"Why not?" Molly cut him short.

"Because . . . we've both changed."

Molly forced a laugh. "How would you know?"

"I hear it in your voice. You're . . . I don't know . . . tougher."

"What do you expect?" Molly said. "Of course, I'm tougher. It came with the . . . the deception."

There was quiet for a moment, then James lamented, "Please don't hate me, Molly."

"Hate? I do hate! I hate what you *did!*"

"Me too. I've hated every moment of it. Please believe me."

Molly groaned, putting her face into her free hand. The conversation, though brief, had sapped her energy. "I never got married, James," she said softly.

"I know, or I used to know that, anyway."

"How?"

"I . . . I kept track of you through my parents."

"I can't believe . . ." Molly stammered. "You didn't! You couldn't do such a thing!"

James fought back tears. "I'm sorry . . . I just wanted to know you were all right."

Molly sighed. "Did you always think I was?"

"Sort of," he said. "Pretty much."

"Little did you know," Molly said sadly. "I can't stand this. It's all so wrong."

"We shouldn't meet," James argued. "I don't think we can manage all this."

Molly snorted. "You can't just call me up, step into my life for five minutes, then disappear again. That, I can't handle. We have to meet. Tomorrow. Just tell me where. I'm in Victor, Montana, south of Missoula."

"I'm . . . I'm not a very good driver, so . . ."

"Coeur d'Alene, then. Where in Coeur d'Alene?"

Thinking fast, James decided the darker the place, the better.

"Uh, there's a café downtown called The Basement. It's actually in a basement. Do you know it?"

"I'll find it. What time?"

"Um, two o'clock."

"I'll be there."

"I . . . I hope you can . . . accept . . ."

"I can. Just be there."

"I don't look the same, Molly. I'm—"

"Neither do I! Just be there!"

"OK. Um, good-bye, then."

"No good-byes, James. I'll see you tomorrow."

"Tomorrow," he said, hanging up.

Molly kept the receiver to her ear, listening to the dead line. Finally her eyes focused on Stephanie, whom she had forgotten was present.

Stephanie's face had turned white as a sheet.

"Am I dreaming?" Molly asked, trembling uncontrollably.

Stephanie shook her head. "I don't think so."

Molly set the phone on the table, releasing herself to cry. Instead of tears, however, a throbbing flooded her head and chest, and all she could do was moan.

CHAPTER TEN

Making It Through the Night

"He's disfigured, Steph."

Stephanie nodded.

"Did I . . . did I do all right?" Molly asked, handing the receiver to Stephanie.

Stephanie hung up the phone. "You did great!" she said, coming back to give Molly a hug. "Under the circumstances, you were incredible!"

"Thank you," Molly whispered as Stephanie embraced her. She could feel the love. "There was so much more to say."

"Don't be so hard on yourself!" Stephanie stood up. "You'll get your chance tomorrow."

Molly put a hand on her forehead. "I don't know how I'll make it through the night! There's so much to think about, so much to . . . to consider. My mind's reeling!"

"Mine too," Stephanie said, "but we'll take it one step at a time, and we'll be OK."

"Yes," Molly agreed, her face brightening. "We've made a lot of headway, haven't we? We've gotten some good news."

"We have."

"James is alive, Steph!" Molly lifted her hands skyward.

"It's a miracle."

"And we're not going to ruin your vacation!"

"No, unless the house burns down," Stephanie said with a shrug.

Molly rolled her eyes. "I wish you hadn't reminded me."

"Sorry," Stephanie said, sitting down at the table. "So, then, what about tomorrow? You wanna go alone?"

Molly shook her head. "No, you ride along, OK?"

"OK, but speaking of the fire—"

"It won't burn the house down before we get back, Steph. Besides, we'll take a couple boxes of stuff in the trunk of the car, and you can put your clothes in a suitcase to take along. If the fire's worse when we get back, we'll pack my old Escort, too, and we'll haul out some furniture."

"You've got good insurance, right?"

Molly nodded. "Pretty good. My main concern right now is meeting with James—and there's no insurance for that, except what God gives me. So, come along. But I'll see James alone, if you don't mind. It's . . . well . . ."

Stephanie shrugged. "No need to explain; I understand. I'll just hang out or whatever."

"We're meeting downtown in a café, so you can browse the shops," Molly suggested.

"That's fine. Maybe I'll buy you a birthday cake since I haven't even thought about making one."

Molly's eyes grew bigger. "This is too unreal, Steph. I'm meeting James on my birthday!" She let out a little, halfhearted screech. "I'm just so . . . flabbergasted."

Stephanie, sharing in the astonishment, reached across the table and patted Molly's hand. "You know, God works in mysterious ways. All things work together for good to those who love the Lord."

"I hope so," Molly said. She closed her eyes for a second, then focused on the poetry book lying on the table where she had left it. She picked it up and cracked it open.

"Jonathan Roseland wrote a beautiful book, didn't he?" she quipped. Her eyes locked on a poem titled "Sunset Football."

> Bell wires bound the slaughter,
> shadow casting a pint-sized field.
> Rusted swing sets,

crippled and pastured,
shepherd star-minded schoolboys
kicking hungry footballs
over makeshift uprights.
Tug-of-war T-shirts
march across the turf,
smeared in routinely churned mud,
running to daylight until
the final, blinding tackle is made.

The adjacent photograph depicted two little kids, dirty from tops to bottoms, pulling at opposite ends of a rope.

Molly showed the picture to Stephanie. "James and me," she said with a whimper. "Can you believe it? James is alive!" Then she closed the book.

James stood before his bathroom mirror, looking at himself as he thought Molly would. He stared at his droopy left eye and the watery discharge suspended on the lower lid. Repulsed, he let out a phony laugh, then tried to pucker his plastic lips for a kiss.

"Not bad," he jeered when the lips did not move. "Aren't I a dreamboat? A real Prince Charming." He pulled off his wig and tossed it on the counter, then removed his prosthetic ear and dropped it in the sink.

"There," he said, unable to see clearly through his tears but knowing what he looked like. "Isn't that even better, Molly? Don't you . . . don't you want to hug and kiss me?"

He turned from the mirror and limped into the hallway. Having left his cane at his desk, he stumbled to his bedroom door and grasped the doorknob for support.

"Aren't I the graceful one? Perhaps you'd like to dance with me, Molly." He let go of the door, careened toward his bed, but fell short, cracking his head on a bedpost before hitting the floor. The blow dazed him, and as he rolled onto his back, he imagined Bill Bayliss grinning at him with a bullet in his neck. Then he beheld pieces of his own flesh floating beside him in bloody water. He tried to right himself, but a blast resounded to his left. A burning sensation struck his left side, paralyzing him. He held his breath as his body sank below the water's surface.

"No more!" he cried, snapping out of it. He sat up and reached for the bedpost. Grabbing it, he hoisted himself onto the end of the bed. He sat there and fingered the knot on the right side of his forehead.

"Great. Now I'm lopsided."

Kelly appeared at the bedroom door, and James called her to him. He curled his fingers around her green collar. "You stick with me no matter what, don't you, girl?" He gave her a loving shake.

Kelly looked at him with doting eyes.

"Thank goodness for dogs," James said, falling back on the bed. He knew he should ice his bruise, but at the moment he didn't care. He just wanted to lie there and catch his breath, or better yet, his sanity.

Then his head began to pound.

Climbing out of bed, he grumbled, "It's gonna be a rough night."

CHAPTER ELEVEN

The Morning

By nightfall, the Lolo fire had stalled and smoldered after burning a hundred and fifty acres. Firefighters and the helo crew had left the mountain, confident that an early morning return would find the fire still docile.

The Gash Peak blaze, however, was anything but pussyfooted. After boiling all afternoon, the fire had swallowed another mile of landscape. Twenty firefighters, including two women, had been ordered to remain on the mountain throughout the night, digging line with their Pulaskis and combies via light from their headlamps. The fast-paced excavation method involved ten ground crew with Pulaskis in single file, with the first person tearing into the rocks or tree roots of the first layer of sod with one wallop before stepping ahead and swinging again while the second one followed behind, cutting into and expanding the holes. He or she was followed by the third, and so on. After ten hits at the same patch of earth by the first line, the ten crew members wielding combies moved up, digging a two-foot wide trench in the Pulaski-softened dirt. A mile of fire line right down to mineral soil was dug in two hours. Then another mile. The hope was that when the broad fire front reached the ditch, it would die from lack of fuel.

Things looked good at dawn; the fire had constricted in the cool night air. Some of the firefighters grinned as the petering flames met the trench with merely a hiss, and they beat each little flare-up with Pulaskis and combies as though smashing the head of a snake. But a strong gust of wind kicked up from the west, fanning a segment of the burn on the hill above the crew into a more active blaze. The firefighters saw three spot fires, launched ahead of the main fire by way of sparks in the breeze, burning a quarter mile outside their fire line. When the crew looked back above them, flames were surging down the ridge in pulses. Then the spot fires grew together. Within minutes, the flame front was half a mile long. The firefighters were forced to hike down the mountain to safety.

Molly found herself uncharacteristically in the kitchen at 6:00 A.M. She had been up and dressed in a pair of beige slacks and a white blouse for more than an hour, waiting impatiently for Stephanie to wake. While she prepared breakfast, she looked out the window numerous times at the smoke rising from over the mountain to the west. The sunrise lit the swelling mushroom cloud with lavender, yellow, and burnt orange hues, spawning a strangely bewitching sight.

When Stephanie finally showed herself in her pajamas, Molly complained, "It's about time!"

Stephanie hooted. "Look who's banging the pans like cymbals now!"

"Don't start!" Molly warned, flipping a pancake. "I only got two hours of sleep."

"Gotcha," Stephanie said with a grin. She slid a chair out from the table. "Need any help?"

"No, just sit down."

Stephanie sat and watched Molly work, admiring her gracefulness and beauty. She wondered what James would think of her, then answered her own question out loud.

"James is gonna be amazed at how young you look for a forty-nine-year-old."

Smirking, Molly said, "Is that your way of telling me 'Happy Birthday'?"

Stephanie chuckled. "Sorry! I can do better than that. Happy Birthday, Moll."

Molly carried a plate with a half dozen pancakes to the table. "Here you go, and thanks anyway for the compliment."

"You're welcome, and thanks for the breakfast," Stephanie said. She took three pancakes, buttered them thoroughly, and smothered them in maple syrup.

"How 'bout if you pray?" Molly suggested after sitting down.

"Sure." Stephanie bowed her head. She meditated for a moment, then petitioned, "Dear Lord, thank you for this day and this meal. Watch over and guide us as we travel to Coeur d'Alene, and especially be with Molly. Give her courage and peace. And please protect human life from the fire. In Jesus' name I pray. Amen."

Stephanie took her knife and fork and began cutting up her pancakes. "So, it takes four hours to get to Coeur d'Alene?"

Molly reached for the syrup bottle. "Almost."

"That means," Stephanie said, doing the math, "we have to leave by ten o'clock, right?"

"Actually, it's an hour earlier over there, but I'm too nervous to wait, Steph. Let's go as soon as we can."

"No problem," said Stephanie, taking a bite. "I need a bath, though."

Molly smiled. "Make it quick. Don't lounge around, admiring the view through the skylight."

Stephanie fluttered her eyelids.

"Just kidding. I'll do the dishes while you get ready. I need to stay busy."

"Gotcha."

"Of course, I was busy all night, tossing and turning. What torture!"

"I'll bet," Stephanie said.

"Yeah, and you slept like a log, right?"

Amused, Stephanie replied, "Not unless a log dreams."

"Oh, yeah? What'd you dream about?"

"Love, I guess."

"Love?"

Stephanie forked a chunk of pancake. "I called Phil last night before I went to sleep, and I dreamt about him."

"Huh," Molly said crankily. "Well, I called Tom around midnight."

Stephanie had opened her mouth, ready to take a bite, but she stopped short. "Hathaway?" she inquired. "Why?"

"Why not? He seems to care a lot."

"Yeah, but you've turned him down for a date three times!"

Molly's eyes flashed. "How do you know?"

"He told me!"

"Well, he's a nice man, that's all. I needed someone to talk to."

"I'm always available, Moll."

"You were asleep, and besides, we talked mostly about the fire."

"Did you tell him about going to see James?"

"Yes, I did."

"What'd he say?"

"It was the right thing to do, and he wished me well."

"And?"

"He told me to give James a chance to explain himself."

"Sounds like good advice."

Molly gave a halfhearted smile. "Yeah, well, the first thing I'm gonna ask him is how well he slept last night."

"Poorly, no doubt," Stephanie wagered.

"That had better be the case," Molly said, jabbing her fork into a pancake. "If he rested easily, then he's not the man I loved."

Stephanie raised her eyebrows and nodded. Glancing toward the kitchen window, she asked, "So, how's the fire?"

Between bites, Molly said, "It's still far away, over the top of the mountain. I'm not going to worry until Cliff knocks on the door and tells me we're in danger."

"Yeah, but we won't be home all day to know if he comes," Stephanie protested.

"I'm sure he'll leave a note. And when we come back, the size of the fire in the night sky will tell us all we need to know."

When James awoke, he looked at the bedroom clock.

"Nine-fifteen!" he bellowed, throwing off his blanket. "It's late!"

Kelly stood up at the side of the bed.

"Good morning, girl." James put his feet on the floor beside the dog and stroked her forehead. "I know you don't need to go outside 'cause you just came in a couple hours ago!" He took his cane and headed for the bathroom. Kelly followed him.

"Some night, hey, Kelly?" The poet, clad only in his shorts, waddled to the bathroom sink and looked at himself in the mirror. The bump on his forehead was black and blue. His eyes were bloodshot and tired.

This is it, he told himself. *A face-to-face encounter with the only woman I've ever loved. Her face and my facade. Molly and my mask. Her truths and my lies. How am I going to survive this? If she despises me . . . if she rejects me . . . how will I go on?*

He left the bathroom and ambled down the hallway toward the kitchen. Along the way, he looked at the picture hanging on the wall.

"Molly," he whispered, admiring the photograph taken three decades earlier of the nineteen-year-old brunette. "So beautiful . . ."

Shaking his head, he went to the kitchen and made a cup of instant coffee. He carried the cup to his desk. As he sat down, he noticed a whitetail deer standing just outside his wooden fence. He looked closer and saw it was a doe, but it was too far away to distinguish anything else.

Maybe it's No Fear, bringing me a message: "Buck up. Get a grip."

James drank some coffee and eyed his typewriter. He put down the cup and dropped in a piece of paper. His fingers hit the keys.

TO MOLLY

I promised I would love you
forever and a day,
then I loved you for a year
and threw the rest away.

I buried all our dreams
at the bottom of a creek,
where a fire burned my honor
and the future you still seek.

Eight and twenty years have gone,
lost because of me;
you not knowing why,
but now you shall see.

"But now you shall see," James mumbled under his breath before shouting, "Now you shall see!" He yanked the paper out of the typewriter and tore it in two.

CHAPTER TWELVE

The Meeting

As James drove his truck to downtown Coeur d'Alene at 1:30 in the afternoon, his body was shaking. He could not remember a time in his life when he was more afraid, and that included his near-death experience in Vietnam. Back then he had confronted physical death via an enemy keen on destruction; now, through one he had loved, he knew he possibly faced emotional and even spiritual death. *This is scarier,* he thought.

On Sherman Street, the main thoroughfare of Coeur d'Alene, he kept his eyes peeled for a vehicle with Montana license plates as he approached The Basement on the corner of Sherman and Fifth. He spotted a van, but the only occupant he saw was an elderly male driver.

Bypassing the restaurant, James drove to the clock tower at the bottom of the hill where the road skirted Lake Coeur d'Alene and the resort motel on the water's edge. He parked his truck on Lakeside Drive next to the tower and walked out on the dock where a couple dozen seagulls had gathered. Some of the birds flew away as he hobbled in his cowboy boots across the wooden planks, thumping with his cane. Most of the birds simply hopped aside, cautious yet still looking for a handout.

James dug a piece of chewing gum out of his jeans pocket, unwrapped it, and quartered it. He tossed the pieces in four directions, causing a rush all around him.

I always seem to provoke a stir, and today will be no exception. This time, though, it could kill me.

He started to walk away, but a seagull skittered in front of him, watching his every move.

"Sorry, ol' boy," James said. "There's nothing else."

The gull hesitated, then skipped aside.

"No food, no friend," James mused aloud. He walked farther onto the dock and sat on a small, concrete bench. The bench felt warm in the eighty-degree afternoon heat. He took several deep breaths, removed his cowboy hat, and turned his face toward the sun. A sailboat caught his attention as it drifted past, about fifty meters from the end of the dock. Squinting hard against the glistening of the water, he watched the man and woman on the boat kiss.

Lucky people. I wish I were so fortunate.

He tipped his head back and basked for a few minutes in the warmth of the sun, calming himself down. Finally, he got up and trudged back to his truck. When he started the engine and looked up the hill toward the café, his hands began to tremble. Slowly, he drove to the corner of Sherman and Fifth and parked directly across the street from The Basement.

After giving himself a little time to work up his nerve, James took his cane and shuffled to the restaurant entrance. His eyes and good ear were on full alert as he anticipated a sudden encounter.

Reaching for the doorknob, James nearly jumped out of his skin when the café door swung open and two middle-aged women stepped toward him.

"Excuse us," said one while James gawked at them. Deploring his stare, the women frowned and walked quickly down the sidewalk away from him.

"I can't do this!" James groaned under his breath. He turned toward the street, wanting to make a mad dash to his truck despite his limitations. He stretched his cane and crippled leg out as far as he could and sprang forward. With three lunges, he barged into traffic and nearly got hit by a car. Drivers from both directions braked their vehicles as he proceeded across the road.

Inside his truck, he fumbled for the keys, not remembering where he had put them. Finally discovering them on the floor beneath his seat, he inserted the wrong key into the ignition. Frustrated, he found the correct key and started the engine.

Before he could drive away, he had to wait for a car to pass by. In that moment, he saw two women walking along the opposite side of the street. His heart leaped in his chest.

"Molly," his mouth formed the word. He watched her enter the café as Stephanie crossed Fifth Street and continued walking down Sherman toward the lake. He shut off the truck and sat paralyzed, unsure of his next move.

Molly stopped at the Please Wait to Be Seated sign at the bottom of the stairs. She was glad to stand still and give her eyes a chance to adjust to the dim basement lighting.

The hostess, a young blonde woman, approached Molly after a short wait. "Just one?" she inquired.

"Actually, I'm looking for a man. He's my age. Do you know if he has already been seated?"

"Don't believe so, but I'll take a look." The hostess disappeared around a wall, only to come back seconds later.

"No single men at all," she said.

Molly checked her watch. "Well, he should be here any minute, so I'll get a table for us."

"Smoking or non?"

"Non," Molly answered. She followed the hostess to a corner booth and sat down, setting her purse on the seat beside her. The hostess handed her two menus.

"Anything to drink while you wait?"

Noticing the liter of ice water already on the table, Molly shook her head. "Water is fine, thanks."

"Your waitress will check on you in a few minutes."

"Oh . . . wait," Molly stopped her. "My friend's name is James."

"James," the hostess said, nodding her head. "I'll watch for him." She left Molly alone.

With unsteady hands, Molly poured herself some water, wincing when two ice cubes bounced off the rim of the glass, launched across the table and landed on the opposite seat. Embarrassed, she looked up to see if anyone had noticed, but no one looked her way.

She slid out of her seat to pick up the ice, noting the weakness in her legs. The first cube slipped out of her fingers and fell to the floor beneath the table, so she simply whisked the other off the seat too.

I'm so nervous, she told herself, sitting back down. *I wish he'd get here.* She raised her glass to her lips, spilling water down her chin. She wiped her face with a napkin.

"Help me, Lord," she whispered. She looked around the room again, finding no one paying attention to her. Two women in the nearest booth were engrossed in conversation, and an older couple with a little boy seated across the room were busy eating.

Molly peered at her watch. It showed 3:07, but she had not moved the hands back an hour when she entered the Pacific Time Zone. She unstrapped the watch, changed the time, and fastened it back on her wrist.

"Two-oh-seven," she muttered. Stating the time out loud made James's tardiness seem even more inexcusable. *How could he possibly make me wait?*

Molly fidgeted for another couple of minutes before a waitress came to her table.

"Ready to order?"

"Not yet," Molly said. "I'm waiting for someone."

"OK, just call me when you're ready."

Molly held up a finger. "Do you mind if I take a walk for a few minutes?"

"Sure, go ahead. I'll keep your table for you."

Molly grabbed her purse and scooted out of the booth. "Thank you. I'll be right back."

James had been watching the door to the café for ten minutes, ever since Molly went inside. He knew he was wrong not to go after her, but he was immobilized by fear. He could neither face Molly nor flee the scene, so he just sat.

With his eyes tiring and blurring, James closed them and wiped the teardrops from his droopy eye. When he opened them again, he shuddered at the sight of Molly standing outside the restaurant. She appeared to be looking right at him, though a second later she turned and began walking. She took but a few steps, stopping to look at the window display of the art gallery adjacent to the café.

James gripped his door handle and waited.

Is she leaving? Is she upset? Will she go back inside the café?

Suddenly, Molly spun on her heel and marched down the sidewalk away from the gallery and restaurant. James observed her for a moment, then jerked open his door. Without thinking, he pitched himself onto the pavement, leaving his cane on the seat. He held up his hands to stop traffic as he staggered across the roadway.

Reaching the curb, he spotted Molly almost a block away, walking quickly, almost uncatchable. He took a breath to yell for all he was worth.

"Molly!" he cried just as his crippled foot tripped over the curb. He tumbled to the sidewalk, his flailing arms knocking off his cowboy hat and wig. He rolled over once, then sat up and squinted toward Molly. She had stopped and turned around.

"James?" she called, moving toward him.

James saw the wig and hat lying on the sidewalk as he frisked his bald head. He lunged for the wig, but it was just out of reach. He let out a groan.

Molly ran up to him, halting abruptly ten feet away. She looked thunderstruck.

James lowered his eyes, helplessly exposed.

CHAPTER THIRTEEN

And Miles to Go . . .

"James," Molly said softly, taking a step toward him. He held up his hands to stop her, then struggled to stand up. A burly man, who had approached from behind James, hooked him by his armpits and hoisted him to his feet.

"Gosh!" the man grunted when James turned to face him. "What happened to you?"

James didn't answer. He bent down and picked up his hat and wig, wishing he could disappear.

"James," Molly spoke again, and James knew he could hide no longer. There would be no more delays and no taking cover. Because of his sprawl on the sidewalk, he was not even afforded a partial disguise. This was it: total revelation.

As the brawny Good Samaritan sauntered off, James looked at Molly. He attempted a sheepish grin, but it didn't feel right, so he wiped it away.

"Your face said it all," James spoke directly, his lisp accentuated. He felt his knees knocking.

Molly frowned at him. "What's that supposed to mean?"

"I saw the horror in your eyes when you came up to me," he said, slapping the cowboy hat on his head. The hat was too big without the wig, so he took it off and tossed the wig inside the crown. "You heard that guy's reaction. That's why I left you alone all these years."

Molly moved closer. "I admit I stopped short a minute ago, and I'm . . . I'm dismayed by what's happened to . . ."

"To my face," James blurted. "To my head, my hair, my eye, my—"

"Stop it!" Molly said, turning away.

"I'm repulsive!" He took a step back.

Molly wheeled toward him. "What are you doing?"

"I'm leaving," he said, beginning to walk.

Rushing alongside him, Molly said, "No way!" She grabbed his shoulder, bringing him to a standstill. The touch sent a shiver through both of them.

"Listen, if anyone walks away, it'll be me," Molly said, removing her hand. "You don't have the right to do it again!"

James tried to look away, but the flash in Molly's eyes magnetized him. In an instant he was enveloped by her glow and her will, melting him to the core. It was just like the first time he had met her.

For a moment, James forgot who he was. He forgot his mutilation; he forgot his lies; he forgot the lost years. He only beheld Molly, and her beauty was so engrossing that he felt beautiful, too, just standing in her aura. He felt new. Uplifted. Alive.

"Look, Mommy!" a child said, walking by. James saw a woman ushering two little girls away from him, and just like that, he snapped back to reality.

"You're so pretty," he said to Molly, "and I'm . . . a beast." Tears filled his eyes, and he hid his face in his hat.

Molly held her breath, feeling at a loss. Then, overcome with compassion, she put her arms around James and pulled him close. His tears were warm on her neck as she hugged him.

For a brief moment James lost himself in Molly's embrace. Then, just as quickly, he felt awkward, undeserving of Molly's tenderness. He tried to back away, but Molly held on. Her fervor stirred him. For the first time in years, the poet actually felt *alive*.

Molly was clinging to a fantasy, and she knew it. She wanted to believe the old James, her fiancé, was in her clasp, but she knew when she released him from the hug she would be dealing with a different man. A changed man. The thought of it chilled her, and she felt afraid.

"I have a table for us in the restaurant," Molly finally said, letting go. She looked into James' languid eye and stifled the impulse to cringe.

Tenderly, she touched his elbow and turned him toward the café. "Let's go sit down."

James hesitated. "First tell me if I get this on right," he said, planting the wig on his head and awkwardly trying to adjust the hair until it felt OK. He then waited for Molly's assessment.

"Looks good to me," she said, though her statement felt vaguely dishonest.

James shoved his cowboy hat down over the wig. "I'll go with you, Molly, but I'll understand if you end up hating me."

"Don't jump the gun." She grasped his arm and led him to the café entrance.

"I don't walk very well," James said, stating the obvious.

"The war?"

"A grenade blast shattered my hip. I've got a cane in my truck."

"Don't worry," Molly said, opening the café door, "lean on me." She helped James navigate the stairs, then steered him to her table. The same people who had ignored Molly earlier now were watching intently.

"It's me," James said, sensing Molly's perturbation. "They always stare at me." He sat down in the booth, and Molly sat in the seat opposite him.

"Then again," James continued, "maybe this time they're staring at you. I've forgotten what it's like to be with a beautiful woman who turns heads."

Molly's cheeks flushed. "Well," she said, "you haven't forgotten how to dish out a compliment."

"That's amazing, really, since I have so little contact with anyone."

Molly, having noticed the rigidity of James' lips, did not want to gawk like the other people. She picked up the glass of water she had poured earlier and took a drink.

This is all so unreal. What do I say? How do I look at him? Where on earth do we go from here?

James took the pitcher of water and shakily poured himself a glassful. With glass in trembling hand, he said, "This may not be pretty. Sometimes I get more on my face than in my mouth."

"No big deal," Molly said. "You should've seen me fifteen minutes ago spilling ice cubes on the floor and water down my chin."

"Sounds just like me," James related. He drank from his glass, spilling nary a drop.

For the next several seconds, a curtain of silence fell between them. Neither was interested in further small talk. The gravity of their situation was obvious, yet both were fearful to address it. As their anxiety grew, however, each realized that even a hit-and-miss approach would be better than dead air.

"Um, may I ask you something?" Molly blurted. She felt her heart racing. James nodded, lowering his gaze.

"Why did you publish . . . my poems?"

James winced. "That's a tough one." He swallowed what felt like a brick. "I sent some poetry, new poetry, to Fawnhaven Publishers and . . . for some reason I included three I had written for you. They were the only three I had copies of." He looked at Molly. She blinked and looked away.

"I think, maybe, it was just a tribute to what we once had," he said, drawing Molly's eyes back to him. "The words were heartfelt, and I thought they deserved to be in the book."

"That's it?" Molly whined. "The *words* deserved recognition?"

"What do you mean?"

"You thought your words were worthy to be . . . resurrected . . . to be preserved and noticed . . . but you were content to leave me buried and forgotten?"

James winced. "No, that's not it. It wasn't only about the words. I thought . . . maybe by including the poems, something good might happen."

"Like what?" Molly challenged.

"Really, I had no idea. Just something . . . *Anything* good, for once."

"Were you crying out for something? Reaching out?"

Shaking his head, James said, "I don't think so."

"Were your reaching out to me? To God? To—"

"To God?" James wrinkled his forehead. "I don't know about that."

"Why not?"

"I don't think God's been very good to me."

Molly's heart sank. She bit her lip, then asked quietly, "Have you been good to God?"

Taken aback, James sighed. He hadn't prepared himself for a discussion centered around deity. "I haven't thought much about it," he mumbled.

"You haven't thought much about it?" Molly leaned in. "You write a book called *Glimpses of Love and Life* and haven't thought much about God?"

"That's not what I said," James replied, narrowing his eyes. "I said I haven't thought much about how good I've been to God."

Molly nodded. "OK. So, you've thought a lot about the Lord?"

James shrugged. "You can't help but think about him when bullets are flying by your head. Or when your best friend gets killed right in front of your eyes. Or when your body gets blown to bits and set on fire, and you should've died but didn't."

"Or when you're told your fiancé is dead and you realize all your dreams died with him!" Molly interjected in a raised voice, causing James's countenance to fall. "That's when I had some serious thoughts about God."

"And you didn't think very highly of him, did you?" he said defensively.

"No, not for a while, but it turns out I was wrong to be angry at him for letting you die, doesn't it?" Her stare was severe.

James fumbled with his water glass before getting it to his mouth. After a swallow, he muttered, "Well, *I'm* still angry at him for *not* letting me die."

"I see," Molly said. "So that's why you haven't been good to God?"

James set down his glass, fighting a drowning sensation. "I haven't been anything to him, neither good nor bad. I'm nothing to him."

"I disagree," Molly said, speaking softly. "God loves you."

James shook his head. "Nobody loves me, Molly. Nobody."

"I can't believe that."

"Only Kelly," he said.

"Kelly? Who's that?"

James's manner softened a bit. "She's my Irish setter."

"A dog! The one mentioned in your book! Where is she?"

"Home, waiting for me, no doubt."

"Then that makes two who love you," Molly said.

"Two?"

"Kelly and God."

James looked down at the table.

"And what about your dad?" Molly asked, pressing ahead.

James picked up a napkin to dab his eye. "He's remarried and living in Orlando."

"I know. I'm sorry about Mary."

"He hasn't talked to me since her funeral. I didn't go."

Nodding, Molly said, "I was there."

"I swore my parents to secrecy, and when I wouldn't go to the funeral, that was the end for my dad." He looked at Molly, hoping for an expression of sympathy.

"I'm sure he still loves you," Molly replied with a soft smile. "You should go see him and make amends."

"He doesn't want anything to do with me."

"Go see him," Molly repeated. "A father needs his son, and a son needs his father. I'm sure of it."

"I don't know," James said.

"You don't know? You don't know about God's love, and you don't know about your dad's love? All you know is a dog's love! Is that what you're telling me?"

James looked into Molly's wide-open eyes. Boldly, he asked, "What about *your* love?" As soon as the words were out, he knew he had spoken too aggressively.

Struck dumb, Molly grimaced and sat back in her seat. "I . . . I don't know," she said dryly, averting her stare.

James realized that he had leaped into a deep hole. "So now you're the one who doesn't know?" he croaked, scrambling to save himself.

"Under the circumstances, I think it's a little premature to ask about my love, James. You know I loved you."

"That's . . . uh . . . past tense." His throat tightened.

"Is it?" Molly asked, glumly. "I guess it is. But through all these years, I never stopped loving the James Wade I was going to marry."

Tears welled up in James's eyes. He drew a quick breath, then said, "But that's not me, is it?" He used his napkin again as Molly took her time in replying.

Finally, she folded her hands on the table and said, "I don't know what to say . . . except that the man I loved never lied to me before."

James suddenly felt that deep hole cave in around him.

CHAPTER FOURTEEN

Looking Within

Deputy Cliff Casman knocked on the front door of Molly's house in the midafternoon, but no one answered. He intended to inform Molly that a Stage 1/Alert was in effect and to have her fill out an evacuation form, as he had done at a half dozen other homes in the White's Lane area of Victor. The form, included in a fire information packet, was necessary in order for the authorities to keep track of the whereabouts of all endangered residents, for safety purposes.

Cliff decided to leave the packet inside the screen door and return in a couple of hours. As he walked to his patrol car, he looked at the vast cloud looming over the mountain behind Molly's acreage. Since there were twin smoke towers, he deduced that the main fire had split in two as it moved around both sides of Glen Lake.

Opening his car door, Cliff noticed the charcoal gray and white ashes that had sprinkled the windshield and roof. *I've been salted and peppered,* he thought, snickering. He took a swipe at the ashes on the roof, then climbed into the car and drove off.

Meanwhile, the Gash Peak fire had indeed flanked both sides of the lake, which was only three hundred yards across. Forty fire-fighters had returned to a lower position on the mountain and were busy digging a line east of the lake, hoping to contain the blaze before it made a two-mile march toward Smith Creek Drainage. The incident commander and every experienced firefighter knew that if fire ignited in the heavily-fueled drainage, nothing could stop it from racing the final mile toward eight homes on White's Lane. The incident commander also had determined that if the four helicopters and slurry bomber he had authorized did not douse the two veins of fire with water and retardant before the fires merged at the end of the lake, he would initiate a Stage 2/Warning, indicating the probable need for evacuation. At the worst, were the fire to jump the new line being built to the east, he would submit a Stage 3/Request for White's Lane and Iroquois Trail residents to vacate their homes. He would also inaugurate a last-ditch effort to dig a mile-long, thirty-foot-wide firebreak between the homes in Molly's neighborhood and the forest behind them.

A waitress, older and stockier than the one who had served Molly earlier, approached the booth.

"Sorry for the delay, but we were all busy in the kitchen," she said, looking toward Molly.

James wondered if she was telling the truth. He envisioned her and the other employees huddled together and drawing straws for the unlucky duty of waiting on him.

"What can I get you?" the waitress asked Molly.

"Just coffee. I'll need some cream, please."

As she scribbled on her pad, the waitress turned toward James. Without looking up, she asked, "And you, sir?"

"The same," he replied. He scooped up the menus and handed them to the waitress, who barely glanced at his face.

"Thank you," she said, walking away.

James felt like calling her back and asking her to recite the day's lunch specials just to make her interact with him, but as usual, he let her off the hook. *Or perhaps,* he thought, *I'm letting myself off the hook.*

"Notice how everyone treats me?" he asked Molly.

"They're just uncomfortable . . . with your injuries," she said, playing it low-key.

"Are you uncomfortable with my injuries?" he grilled her.

Molly glowered. "Come on, James, I'm uncomfortable with *everything* right now, and so are you, so let's try to move on, OK?"

Rebuffed, James simply nodded his head. He marvelled at the

spunk he saw in Molly and genuinely admired the mature woman she had become.

"I've got a question," Molly forged ahead. "How'd you sleep last night?"

Amused, James snickered. "How'd I sleep?"

"Yes," she said, staying serious. "Good or bad?"

"Bad."

Molly grinned. "That's good."

"Good? I hardly slept at all!"

"Me, too, that's why it's good. If you said you slept like a baby, I'd get up and leave right now."

James eyed her skeptically. "You're serious? In other words, that was a loaded question."

"It was. Here's another loaded question for you."

James sat forward. "If I answer wrongly, I hope the consequences won't be so severe."

She shrugged. "We'll see."

"What's the question?"

"What day is this?" Molly asked, looking him in the eye.

James shrank back a little. "It's Thursday, but that's not the answer you're looking for."

Molly shook her head.

"It's July eighth."

Again, Molly shook her head. She leaned back, expecting him to flounder.

"Well," he said, happy the conversation had turned lighthearted, "the only answer that'll score points is that today's your birthday."

Gladdened, Molly smiled. "Correct! And how old am I?"

James figured for a moment, then offered, "Thirty-six."

"What?"

"Don't try to convince me otherwise," he said, trying to work his lips into a partial grin. "I know thirty-six when I see it."

Molly giggled, and it warmed James's heart. He remembered days when he and Molly had shared love and laughter in seemingly endless waves. But those times were long gone, as were the people they themselves had been. Here they sat, a fifty-one-year-old broken, aggrieved man and the forty-nine-year-old lovely woman he had deceived.

"Happy birthday, Molly," James said softly, "and I'm sorry I wasn't there for so many others."

Molly closed her eyes. "Your not being there, and my believing you were dead, only to discover I've been lied to . . . it all adds up to the fact that you've ruined part of my life. You've totally altered what *should* have been." Molly peered at James, who shamefully dropped his gaze.

There goes the joy, he thought. *Now I pay the piper. I'm finished.*

"A year or two of this deception would've been unforgivable," she continued. "So how can you expect me to excuse a twenty-eight-year sham?"

James shook his head. "I can't," he muttered.

"I don't know what to do or say."

"Me, neither."

Molly fought back tears. "Give me some direction, James. I gave up so much of my life for you. I never married because I wanted only you. I've lived alone, largely unfulfilled, and I would've died if it weren't for God. And now here you are, and I don't feel as much empathy or forgiveness as I hoped I would."

James managed the courage to look up at her. "What *do* you feel?"

Molly wiped her eyes. "I feel . . . loss, and bitterness, I guess. And I'm praying . . . I won't end up rejecting you."

"Like everyone else."

"No, not that way," Molly said quickly. "It's only skin-deep with everyone else. I can handle the scars on your face. Maybe not perfectly, but I can handle it. I wish you could."

The waitress returned with two cups, a creamer, and a small pot of coffee on a tray.

"Here you go," she said, setting the cups on the table, then filling them. She placed the creamer before Molly. "Sugar packets are right there." She pointed at the small bowl on the table.

"May I get you anything else?"

"No, this is fine," Molly said, forcing a smile.

The waitress returned the smile and left.

Molly poured some cream in her coffee, giving James a chance to speak. When he remained silent, she continued with her thoughts. "My problem isn't skin-deep. It's, well, you know what it is—"

"I can't undo what I've done," James said, hating the ring to his own words.

"That's the unfortunate truth." Molly tore open a packet of sugar over her cup, going through the motions, though she was not the least bit interested in the drink.

"Then what can I do?" The rise in his voice gave Molly pause.

Looking at him, she said, "I'm not sure. We've got to figure something out." She dropped the empty wrapper on the table, and before she could pick up her spoon, James leaned forward and clenched her right hand with both of his. The swift action surprised her, making her jump and instinctively pull away. But James's grip was secure.

"Forgive me for ruining your life," he said, drooling as he spoke. He felt the slobber, but for the first time in ages, he let it go. There was no way a little saliva, or anything else, would stop him from an attempt at resolution now that he had made his move.

"Forgive me, then you're free to go and restore your life!" He squeezed her hand tighter before easing off with a gentle caress. "You're only forty-nine, Molly, with years and years ahead of you."

Molly looked at their entwined hands and sighed. "I thought you said I was thirty-six." She took her napkin in her free hand, reached out, and patted his chin.

"Come on, Molly, don't destroy your future by having anything to do with me. Just forgive me, for both our sakes, then go home and find someone who can give you the love you deserve."

Frowning, Molly said, "Easier said than done."

"Which part? The forgiving, or finding someone to love you?"

"Both."

"You can't forgive me?"

Molly pulled her hand away. She resented what she perceived as a sudden dismissal. "I hope I can, but not today," she snapped. "Not right now. I'm too numb, too shocked. I don't know what we're gonna do. Do you?"

"No, it's too complicated. That's why you should walk away."

Molly's gaze grew stern. "I can't believe you! You suggest some quick fix that's no answer at all. It's a cop-out, and I'm offended by it."

"Why?"

"Why?" Molly shook her head in disbelief. "You threw me away and tell me how hard it was. And now you're ready to throw me away again, and you're making it sound easy. I thought our love was greater than that."

"It was!" James said through clenched teeth. "It was special, and I want you to have that kind of love again. But I'm not the one who can give it to you."

"How do you know?" Molly argued. "How are you so sure?"

"Just look at me!" he cried, pointing at his face. "*That's* how I know!"

Molly leaned forward. "Come on, James! That's not the answer!"

"Oh, yeah? Then what is?"

"Your poems—the poems you yourself wrote—they have the answer! Love and joy and hope . . . wonder and caring . . . the stuff that lives on the inside!" She brushed a hair from her cheek and then pointed to her heart. "You've got to look within. Inside. That's where it counts."

James put his face in his hands, wanting desperately to believe her.

CHAPTER FIFTEEN

Cupid

Stephanie walked up and down Sherman Street, window-shopping in a halfhearted way. She was worried about Molly.

After wandering back to The Basement and loitering on the sidewalk for several minutes without a glimpse of her friend, Stephanie, like millions before her, felt drawn to the lake down the hill. She set off, power-walking the five blocks. Unbeknownst to her, she ended up resting on the same concrete bench where James had sat. Many of the same seagulls vied for her attention.

When Stephanie produced none of the usual treats, the birds lost interest in her and flitted away. Stephanie's thoughts turned inward. She became aware of how hard her heart was beating, mostly due to the exercise, she knew, but anxiety was a factor too. She pictured Molly and James sitting in the restaurant, holding hands and falling in love again.

Wishful thinking, Stephanie thought, then she visualized the couple angrily locking horns.

Bowing her head, she prayed, "Please God, may your will be done between Molly and James, and help me be there for Molly—"

"Excuse me!"

Startled, Stephanie looked up into the unshaven, leathery face of an old man.

"You're on my bench, missy." The face was pockmarked, the eyes bloodshot, and for a fleeting moment Stephanie thought it was James.

"It's three o'clock," he said in a raspy voice, motioning for her to move. "Everyone knows it's my time."

As he inched closer, Stephanie noted the threadbare flannel

shirt, the grungy jeans with holes in the knees, and torn sneakers. She surmised that this man was a derelict.

She stood up.

"You're the slowest one yet, little lady," he said, slinging a stuffed, worn backpack onto the bench. "What's wrong? Got the weight of the world on your shoulders?"

Stephanie backed away, then remembered her purse sitting on the bench. She moved toward it, but the man sat down, stalling her.

"Have a seat," he said, pointing to the wooden planks of the dock. He raised a bristly eyebrow and flashed a gap-toothed grin.

"Well, I've, ah—"

"Go on," he insisted, "take a load off. My name's Cupid. Lemme cheer you up." He smiled again and patted his oily, matted hair.

Stephanie wondered if she had heard him correctly. "Cupid?"

"Yeah, gotta minute?" he asked in a softer tone.

Stephanie thought of Molly and James, and wondered if James was as unsightly as this "Cupid."

Molly would sit, Stephanie told herself, so she tentatively seated herself at the vagrant's feet.

"So how are you gonna cheer me up?" she asked, still a little nervous.

"Watch," he said, reaching into his pocket. He brought out a plastic bag and waved it in front of Stephanie.

"Bird seed," he stated. He opened the bag and began scattering seeds on the dock. Within seconds, a seagull showed up.

"Come on, my little mateys!" He tossed more seeds into the air and laughed as several birds darted in for the treat.

"I spread love," he said, "and that cheers ev'rybody up, see?"

Stephanie smiled. A gull pecked heartily beside her.

"They look pretty happy," she admitted.

"They love my poetry too," Cupid said, dumping the last of the seeds before stuffing the empty bag into his pocket.

"You're a poet?"

Cupid grinned. "A man of many talents, specializing in those that cheer people up. That includes poetic recitations."

Stephanie began to relax. "Can you recite something now?"

"I was fixin' to," he said. He snapped his fingers as if to command attention from the seagulls, then tipped back his head.

"Lovely, lovely, lovely is the bright, sunny day; sittin', sittin', sittin' on the dock of the bay. Time, time, time is a-flyin' by the way; my, my, my, how I wish that it'd stay."

He paused to lick his lips. "Sweet, sweet, sweet are the birds on the wing; hi, hi, hi is the message that they sing. Yes, yes, yes, do they love what I bring; no, no, no, I'm a pauper, not a king!"

He glanced at Stephanie with a twinkle in his eye. She reacted with obligatory applause.

"That was very good," she said.

"I wrote it for my friends." He gestured toward the bustling birds. "That's Whitey over there on the left. The real white one."

"He's cute."

"And that's Hopscotch further out, jumping around."

Stephanie nodded.

"So, pray tell, what's your name?"

Stephanie looked at Cupid, who was squinting at her. "Um, Steph."

"Short for Stephanie?"

She smiled. "Yes."

"That's my brother-in-law's wife's name," he said, grinning. "I always liked her."

He turned his head and gazed out over the lake. "Yep, that's a nice name," he said quietly.

Stephanie realized she still hadn't retrieved her purse, but somehow she was less concerned about it now. Her interest had shifted toward Cupid.

"You are married?" she asked.

His countenance fell. "Was. Her name was Randa. She was killed . . . in a car wreck. My fault."

"I'm sorry," Stephanie said.

"Happened three years ago. Been here ever since."

Stephanie looked around at the birds. "Been where?"

"The park, the dock. The cemetery's just a half mile down the road, on Government Way. Do you know where that is?"

Stephanie shook her head.

"Forest Cemetery. That's where Randa's buried, in the most beautiful spot you've ever seen. Right in the middle under a sixty-foot tree. It's my special place, where my heart is. There's a sign there that says, 'A cemetery exists because every life is worth loving and remembering—always.' I like that."

Nodding, Stephanie said, "It sounds like you were very happy together."

"Randa was a great woman. All I ever wanted was to cheer 'er up."

"I'm sure you did."

"I wrote her a lot of poetry, and I recite some by her grave every night." He watched a seagull inch toward the seeds near his feet. Keeping still, he said, "I sometimes share love poems other people have written too. There are so many beautiful ones."

"Um, you read a lot of poetry?" she asked.

"Yep. Most every day I hang out at Woody's Books. I never get tired of reading poetry."

"Have you seen a book called *Glimpses of Love and Life*?"

Cupid flashed a smile. "Read every page. Now that man knows about love—and sadness."

Amazed, Stephanie blurted, "Well, the author's downtown right now!"

"He is?" Cupid asked, equally astonished. "Where?"

Stephanie immediately regretted her disclosure. Her frown gave her away.

"You know, don't you?" Cupid said excitedly. "Please, take me there."

"I can't do that. He's meeting with a friend of mine."

"So, what time does their meeting end?"

Stephanie shook her head. "You don't understand. There's a lot going on."

"I don't want nothin' from him. I just wanna shake his hand and cheer 'im up, that's all." He leaned toward her. "Pretty please?"

Stephanie tried to think of a way out.

"I recited one of his poems to Randa just last night," Cupid asserted. "I gotta meet him, just for a minute."

Perspiring, Stephanie climbed to her feet. Her movement caused the nearest seagulls to skip farther out.

"May I have my purse, please?"

Cupid handed it to her.

"Nice meeting you," she told him, "and I wish you the very best." She walked away.

Stephanie expected Cupid to shout after her. Instead, his silence swept down the dock and over her like a wave.

Oh, I can't stand leaving him like this, she thought. She suddenly spun around to face him.

"Come on!" she called, not quite believing her own actions.

CHAPTER SIXTEEN

No Ordinary People

"I won't embarrass you," Cupid promised as he walked beside Stephanie up Sherman Street, toting his backpack. Of course, she already was embarrassed by the company of one so unkempt, a fact that made her feel guilty.

Who do you think you are? she scolded herself. *Get down off your high horse. He's just as good as you are.*

She picked her head up and smiled at some passersby. A minute later, however, she fell into a funk. She knew she was out-of-bounds to invade Molly's meeting with James in any way, shape, or form, and that certainly included introducing a stranger into the mix. Still, she was going to do it. She watched her own feet taking one step after another along the sidewalk, making that which was incongruous a reality. She literally saw it happening and was amazed at herself.

Cupid talked nonstop all the way, though Stephanie tuned him out. A few words, like "bug 'im" and "autograph," penetrated her thoughts, but she finally interrupted his "cheer 'im up" speech and told him a little about the fire in Montana just to distract him.

Then, from half a block away, Stephanie saw Molly standing outside the restaurant. A man wearing a cowboy hat stood with her.

Stephanie froze in her tracks, causing Cupid to halt.

"What's up?" he asked. He followed her gaze to the couple. "That them?"

"Just stay behind me," Stephanie said.

Cupid did as he was told as Stephanie walked to the corner of Fifth Street, then crossed and entered Molly's world.

"Steph!" Molly said, surprised.

Molly's escort looked into Stephanie's eyes, and Stephanie saw the disfigurement. She almost gasped, but fought her way to a smile.

"James," she said.

He nodded. "Yes."

"Is this him?" Cupid buzzed, bolting forward.

Molly took a step back from the vagrant, but James held his ground.

"Jonathan Roseland?" Cupid stared at James's face, not flinching a bit. He put out his hand and flashed a wide grin. "Sylvester 'Cupid' Lovingood, at your service."

James hesitated, unaccustomed to such goodwill.

"It's a great honor to meet you, sir," Cupid said.

James saw the sincere face, and he gripped the derelict's hand. They shook firmly.

"I've read your book, Mr. Roseland, and I wanted to tell you how much it means to me and my wife. Thanks for writin' it." Cupid let go of the poet's hand and turned to Stephanie. "Thanks a million, Steph, for cheerin' me up."

He took Stephanie's hand, kissed the back of it, then started away.

"Wait, Cupid!" Stephanie said. "I, uh, want you to meet my best friend, Molly."

Cupid faced Molly. "My pleasure, ma'am. You're lucky to have such a great writer for a husband." He nodded toward James. "And he's lucky to have you. No man could write like that and not be in love."

Molly was speechless.

"OK, gotta go. I promised." With that, Cupid spun on his heel and ambled away.

Stephanie looked after him for a moment, then turned to Molly.

"He begged me, Moll. He's been reciting Jonathan Roseland's

poems at his wife's grave." Stephanie looked at James. "He loves your stuff."

"Cupid?" Molly uttered. "He thought we were married?"

"He's just . . . mixed up," Stephanie said.

Molly shook her head. "Well, he certainly couldn't be further from the truth, Steph. James wants me to forget about him."

James lowered his eyes. Stephanie's scrutiny was too much for him. "I'm sorry you had to find me like this, but it's good to see you, Stephanie," he mumbled.

Stephanie glanced at Molly and raised her eyebrows. Molly pursed her lips, shrugging.

"Well," said Stephanie, "I don't know what's gone on between you two today, but after all these years, James, I could use a hug."

James looked up as Stephanie moved toward him. Her smile broke through his defenses, and a second later he was encircled by her arms. He reacted with a hug of his own.

Molly waited for the embrace to end, then said, "James, do you realize that man, Cupid, idolized you for what's inside you. He didn't care about the scars."

"That makes him one in a million," James replied sheepishly, aware that Stephanie was getting clued in on his insecurities.

Molly inched closer to James as Stephanie shifted her weight away.

"I think there are thousands more just like him," Molly argued. "They'll come to your book signings. You'll see."

"That man's homeless, isn't he?" James asked, looking to Stephanie.

"He basically lives in a park, I think."

"He's down and out, like I am," James insisted. "That's why he relates to me. He's not like ordinary people; he's no stranger to pain."

Shaking her head, Molly said, "James, there are no ordinary people. All of us are peculiar, and we all know pain. Everyone has an outer mask, a coverup. Inside we're all . . . suffocating sometimes."

She brushed James's hand. "Don't suffocate what's in you. You've got a gift."

James stared at his feet. "What's that?"

"Your poems, your viewpoint. Real life. You're touching the pure and lovely things of God, and you don't even know it."

Molly dug into her purse. "One day when you finally realize it, you'll be set free. That's when you'll live out who you really are—the man I fell in love with."

She took a pocket-sized Bible out of her purse and handed it to him.

"This is for you," Molly said, "and I wrote down a few verses I'd like you to read. Call me in a few days after you've thought about them, OK?"

Molly had collared him again. He had made it to within fifty feet of his truck and was a turn of a key away from his reclusion, and now she was soliciting a promise.

"OK," he pronounced before any good excuses came to mind. He tucked the Bible into his shirt pocket. "I guess I'd better go."

Molly maintained a stoic front, but she was anguishing within. Her own words convicted her, *"Everyone has an outer mask, a coverup." How could he have had me come all this way for just an hour and a half? He's so pitiful, so lost. Yet I know there's another James, a wonderful James, deep down inside, chained and unable to come forth. In a prison no one can access—except God.*

"All right," Molly said, giving James a light kiss on the cheek. "I'll wait for your call."

Stephanie hugged him again.

Choking up, he broke away and hobbled across the street. He climbed into his truck, gave a final wave, and drove off.

Molly turned loose her tears.

Ten minutes later, Stephanie drove Molly's car past the clock tower by the lake. Molly, seated in the passenger seat, blew her nose as Stephanie turned the vehicle onto Government Way.

"I think Cupid said it's down here half a mile," Stephanie said, glancing at the signs announcing North Idaho College. She saw some of the educational buildings on her left.

"What'd you think of James?" Molly asked, folding up her tissue.

"I don't know. He wasn't as . . . um . . . maimed as I thought he might be."

"No, not really," Molly agreed, "but you didn't see him without his hair."

Stephanie looked surprised. "You did?"

"Yes, he tripped on the sidewalk and his wig fell off. That's how we met."

"Oh, how awful! I can't imagine. How'd it go after that?"

"Well," Molly said, looking down the road, "I want to say 'not good,' but it wasn't all bad. Both of us expressed ourselves pretty well, I think, and there were some good moments despite the . . . the . . ."

"Upheaval."

Molly smiled. "You got it." After a moment's thought, she added, "Right now I'm just hoping he discovers his true self. May God help him."

"You sound forgiving of what he's done."

Molly looked at Stephanie. "It would take a really big person to forgive him, Steph. I'm afraid I'm too small."

Stephanie pointed ahead. "Right there, Forest Cemetery." She slowed the car and made a left turn onto the garden drive. The cemetery was large, covering several acres. Hundreds of fifty- and sixty-foot pine trees and a seemingly endless number of grave markers filled the landscape.

"What a nice place!" Molly declared.

Stephanie drove past the sign that Cupid had mentioned, reading aloud, ". . . every life is worth loving and remembering—always."

They went up a slight rise, creeping along beneath a shroud of trees.

"I've got to find the middle," Stephanie announced.

"The middle?" Molly questioned, looking back, then forward to gauge their location. "That's a tough guess."

"We'll find it. Women's intuition."

Molly chuckled. "I think this calls for divine direction."

"Start praying, then," Stephanie said with a gleam in her eye, "and let me know when to hit the brakes."

Molly prayed with her eyes wide open, simultaneously craning her neck to get a feel for the layout.

"About fifty more feet," she finally said.

Stephanie looked askance. "Think so?"

Molly waited a few seconds, then said, "Right here."

Stephanie stopped the car. She beheld skyscraper-tall trees all around her.

"What was her name again?" Molly asked.

"Randa. He never said her last name."

Molly opened her door and slid her legs out. "Lovingood. He said his name was Lovingood."

"Was that it?" Stephanie asked, getting out of the car.

"I'm sure that's what he said, so we're looking for Randa, probably Randa Lovingood."

"Under a sixty-foot tree," Stephanie instructed.

Molly looked up between towering trees toward the blue sky. "They all look the same to me!"

"You take that side and I'll look over here," Stephanie said, and the search began.

CHAPTER SEVENTEEN

In the Cemetery

The Lolo fire had been declared 75 percent contained by early afternoon. The fire lines had held, and two crews were working to maintain an established line and to secure the northern perimeter.

The Gash Peak fire, on the other hand, had survived the air assault on both sides of Glen Lake and had blown up on the north-eastern edge of the water, burning so strongly in the afternoon that the combustion energy became similar to a tornado and resulted in fire whirls, creating more heads to the blaze. The spinning, rising columns of hot gases carried black smoke, cinders, and debris high into the sky, forcing the helicopter and slurry bomber pilots to withdraw.

With a lookout intently monitoring the fire's advance, the crews below the lake worked furiously, trying to finish a line they knew wouldn't hold. Still, they had been ordered to get the job done, and they were too close to completion to quit.

The incident commander, having been updated, issued a Stage 2/Warning for residents of White's Lane and Iroquois Trail, totaling seventeen homes.

Molly walked from tree to tree, scanning every gravestone in sight. She was fine for a few minutes, but after a hundred or more markers, her optimism waned.

She looked across the grounds at Stephanie, a hundred yards away, and watched her for a minute. Stephanie's determination was obvious, even at that distance, as she moved briskly and methodically through the monuments.

Dispirited and emotionally spent, Molly stepped behind a tree, out of Stephanie's view, and sat down on a marble tombstone. She no longer wanted to be there, on her birthday no less, reading the names of the dead. She had had enough of that in her life.

She remembered the cemetery back home in Michigan on the shore of Belleville Lake, where she had visited countless times the gravesites of Bill Bayliss, whose body had been buried, and James Wade, for whom a simple stone had been erected. Her bereavement magnified when first her sister, Elise, drowned, and then two years later her mother, Gwen, and father, Marc, both died of cancer within six months of each other. Molly had read all of their names, carved in rock, seemingly a million times until she could take it no longer. She packed her belongings and moved to Montana and the freewheeling West, bound for a new, self-reliant start.

Yet even after four years, Molly had not been successful in detaching herself from life's hardest blows. She remained tied to her past, dwelling on "what could've been" had some vital people lived to love her. Now, incredibly, one of them *had* lived after all, though he hadn't truly loved her. Or had he? He certainly hadn't in a way that she could feel.

She did have the love of God, something her parents had shown her. Both had turned to Christianity during their illnesses, trusting Jesus Christ as Lord and Savior. Together, her mom and dad had shared their newly found faith with Molly, and she had opened her heart and believed. The ensuing love, streaming from heaven, had sustained her. That, and Stephanie.

But she had left Stephanie in Michigan, breaking both of their hearts and adding fresh pain as she sought to cut out the old. They missed each other terribly, and the weekly phone calls and letters over the years helped only a little. Molly's holiday trips to Michigan and Stephanie's summer visits were greatly anticipated and enjoyed, but the parting never seemed to lose its sting. Molly simply had found no one to fill Stephanie's void, and though she hadn't said anything, she was contemplating going back to Ypsilanti and her old teaching job. The position had opened and been offered to her just two days before Stephanie arrived. Molly still had another week to decide.

She looked around the tree trunk and caught sight of Stephanie, who had worked her way closer. Stephanie spied Molly, waved, and continued searching.

I'd better help, Molly decided reluctantly. She stood up and squinted at the headstone to her left.

"Robert Eldon Michael Lemmick," she read aloud before meandering away.

She gazed out over the sea of gravestones and shook her head. *Too many; this is impossible.* When she looked back down, her eyes fell on her own surname on a marble marker.

"Meyers," she uttered. "Lynn A." She read the dates, did the math, and realized this person buried beneath her feet had lived but thirty-three years. Molly wondered whether Lynn Meyers had been a man or a woman, since no other facts had been chiseled.

She stared at the name "Meyers" again, studying each line of each capitalized letter. It was a name she had carried now for forty-nine years, which was twenty-eight years too long, she reckoned.

"Should be Molly Wade." She turned away and resumed checking other gravestones, mumbling as she went.

After a few more minutes, she again wanted to quit. She weakly hailed Stephanie, who didn't hear her. Frustrated, she took several steps toward Stephanie and drew a big breath. But before she could yell, her eyes inadvertently found the prize.

"Randa Fay Lovingood," she sputtered, reading the marker. She raised her head and shouted to her friend, "I found it!"

Stephanie came running.

"Wonderful Daughter and Wife, November 5, 1940, to June 10, 1996," Molly read aloud. "This is it, Steph!"

Stephanie took one look at the hefty, gray marble headstone and gave Molly a hug.

"Thank you."

Molly laughed. "Don't thank me. Thank God. I'd given up."

The women regarded the marker.

"I'm so glad we found it," Stephanie said.

"Me, too, but you never told me why it's so important."

Stephanie smiled. "Because, well, this is the most special place in someone's life, in Cupid's life." She paused a moment to take in the view. "It's pretty here, and he loves it . . . and he loves her."

"He loves her," Molly whispered, "even though she's . . . gone." She bowed her head. "I know how that feels. I loved a dead man for twenty-eight years."

Stephanie stood quietly for a brief time, noting Molly's melancholy. "You OK?" she finally asked.

"I don't know," Molly admitted. "I feel . . . diminished, by what's happened. I'm . . . smaller . . . than I thought I was." She looked into Stephanie's eyes. "I'm accusing James of little and selfish actions, yet I'm afraid I, myself, am too small a person to forgive and maybe love again."

Stephanie took Molly's hand. "Listen, you're the biggest person I know, and your courage is remarkable. Got that?"

Molly looked at the ground.

"Besides, you just got walloped out of the blue, and you're still standing. Whatever's the right thing to do, you'll do it."

Lifting her gaze, Molly formed a smile. "You'd make a great teacher, don't you think?"

Stephanie chuckled. "I wish all my third-graders agreed!"

Molly let go of Stephanie's hand and swatted her arm. "They do, you big dummy."

Stephanie looked back at the gravestone, silently concocting a plan of action. "Tired, Moll?" she asked.

"Yes."

"Why don't you sit under this tree and relax then, and I'll be back in fifteen minutes?"

Molly wrinkled her forehead. "What?"

"Trust me," Stephanie said, bending down and smoothing the grass with her hand. "Just have a seat. I've got something I wanna do, and I'll be right back."

Warily, Molly sat on the ground and watched Stephanie jog to the car, drive out of the cemetery, and head downtown.

What could she be up to? Molly wondered. She lay her head back against the tree and shut her eyes. Breathing deeply, she savored the pine smell, doing her best to close out the rest of the world.

Stephanie came back shortly, though not as quickly as she had promised.

"I couldn't find a grocery," she lamented, carrying a brown paper sack.

Molly got up and brushed the seat of her pants with her hand. "I think I slept for a while. Whatcha got?"

Stephanie grinned. "Stuff for Cupid." She reached into the bag and pulled out a book.

"*Glimpses of Love and Life* from Woody's Books," she announced, waggling it in the air.

Molly shrugged. "It's your money, honey."

"I wrote in the front: To Cupid and Randa from Stephanie." She placed the book on the grave below the headstone.

"That's pretty nice, Steph, considering you haven't signed *my* book yet," Molly needled with a friendly grin.

"Soon," returned Stephanie. Digging a second time into the sack, she came out with a small plastic bag.

"Bird seed!" she said, placing it on top of the book.

"Is Cupid a bird watcher?"

"Seagulls. He considers them his friends." Stephanie moved away from the grave and gave it a final look. "I'm sure he'll find this stuff tonight."

Molly draped an arm around Stephanie's shoulders. "Talk about a big person . . ."

"I just wanted to cheer him up."

Uplifted, the women strolled back to their car—where a store-bought boxed birthday cake sat on the backseat.

CHAPTER EIGHTEEN

Looking to the Heart

James drove home and was met at the front door by his dog.

"Hey, Kelly," he said dispiritedly, unable to match the animal's enthusiasm. He patted her head and let her go outside. Tossing his hat on the couch, he sat down at his desk and put his face in his hands. He could hardly believe he had actually met with Molly after all the lost years, and in retrospect he was disappointed with the meeting—not in Molly, but in himself.

He thought of how beautiful Molly had become, and how foolish he'd been in telling her to forget about him. He realized now that she couldn't do that, any more than he could erase her from his mind. After all, she had never married, even though he knew marriage was something she had wanted twenty-eight years earlier.

He sat back, feeling a bulge in his shirt pocket, and remembered the Bible. He took it out.

Turning to the first page, he read Molly's writing: "Anything worth anything has its worth deep inside, so always look to the heart. The heart of this Book is where I'll lead you—read John 3:16–21; 1 John 5:10–12; 1 Peter 1:23–25; 2:24–25; Romans 8:35–39. Hopefully, Molly."

James had held a Bible in his hands before, but only in his youth. He remembered reading a verse here and there, but he had retained only part of one: "God is love; and he that dwelleth in love dwelleth in God, and God in him." A Sunday school teacher had asked his junior high class, which James had attended less than a dozen times as an eighth grader, to memorize several Scriptures on "love." James studied them just enough to recite them, with frequent prompting, to avoid the teacher's chastisement. Then he quickly forgot about them until years later when he fell head-over-heels for Molly. He had been so filled with love that he surmised God's favor was upon him and running through him. In his euphoria, he had recalled that one particular Scripture and had claimed it as his own.

All was grand for almost a year. Then Vietnam, then the grenade. With the blast went all that James had cherished, but still the Bible verse stuck fast in his head—existing now, it seemed, only to torment him.

"God is love; and he that dwelleth in love dwelleth in God," James mumbled before dropping the Bible on his desk. "I wish . . ." He decided to look up Molly's select Scriptures later in the evening, if he felt like it. Of course, he knew he wouldn't feel like it, but he owed it to Molly. Since she had given him two days, though, there was no rush.

He gave the cover a final look, focusing on the word *Holy.*

Painfully amused, he thought, *I went from holy to holey.* He laughed bitterly, striking the desk with his hand, then hitting it harder and harder with his fist until he collapsed prostrate on the floor. He rolled onto his left side, and the tears streamed from his good eye into his bad. For a moment he relived his good life plunging into his bad life, then he turned face down again, flattening his nose against the floor.

Listening to his restricted breathing, he again thought of Molly.

What if she saw me now? A sniveling, pathetic jellyfish. A coward. A quitter. Is that what I really am?

He rolled onto his back and wiped his eyes. Blinking rapidly, he cleared his vision and stared at the ceiling. Somehow, from who-knows-where, an understanding slowly descended upon him and infused him. He felt lifted, and his nerve center grew acute.

Get up! The words pulsated in his mind like a neon light.

Get up! He raised his head and looked around, knowing the directive went deeper than merely the physical.

Get up! He crawled to his knees, discerning a power pulling at him. He grabbed the edge of the desk and worked his way to his feet. He noticed that the Bible had moved, flipping open during his fall, and his eyes zeroed in on some verses underlined in blue ink.

"He himself bore our sins in his body on the tree, so that we might die to sins and live for righteousness; by his wounds you have been healed. For you were like sheep going astray, but now you have returned to the Shepherd and Overseer of your souls."

As if in a trance, James sat down. A will, superior to his own, had taken charge. There would be no delay. He had to read more—here and now.

"I wonder where he lives, Steph. Where in Coeur d'Alene?" Molly drove her car onto the Veterans Memorial Centennial Bridge, three miles east of the city.

"I have no idea," Stephanie replied, getting a glimpse of Lake Coeur d'Alene before the concrete abutments of the bridge blocked her view.

"Probably not in an apartment. He's got an Irish setter."

"Probably out of town somewhere." Stephanie sat back, seeking to relax. "Did you tell him about the fire?"

"No, I decided not to. It was fire that almost killed him—that *did* kill him, I guess."

"I mentioned the fire to Cupid," Stephanie revealed.

"Maybe he's got a girlfriend," Molly blurted, preferring to talk about James. "He's telling me to forget about him, so maybe he doesn't want me to find out about another woman."

Stephanie guffawed. "He wouldn't do that!"

"You're giving a lot of credit to a guy who's done what he's done to me!"

Hearing the sharp edge to Molly's voice, Stephanie put her head back, closed her eyes, and replied calmly, "Then ask him."

"Ask him what?"

"If there's a mysterious other woman."

Molly didn't like Stephanie's choice of words. She glared at her friend.

Sensing the look, Stephanie said, "You gave him two days to call. When he does, ask him."

"I don't think he'll call."

"I do."

Steamed, Molly trumpeted, "I think I'm just gonna go out with Tom!"

It was Stephanie's turn to give a look. "No, you're not!"

"What? You're the one who's always wanting me to find a man!"

"Well, you found one today. Give it some time to see what happens."

"Easy for you to say! You've got Phil—Mr. Perfect!"

Stephanie took a breath and counted to five. "I know you're stressed, so I'm not gonna respond to your bite."

"My bite?" Molly snapped. "What bite?"

The car exited the bridge, and Molly navigated a sharp curve in the highway.

"We haven't had a fight in a long time. Let's don't have one on your birthday." Stephanie again shut her eyes.

Molly quickly threw out a couple more digs, but when Stephanie remained silent, Molly felt ashamed. She knew the strain she'd been battling had overcome her.

Swallowing her pride, Molly said, "I'm sorry, Steph."

Stephanie smiled softly. "It's OK, Moll, I understand." She peeked out the corner of one eye. "I'm still the best friend you'll ever have, buddy."

Molly chuckled. "Lucky me," she replied, meaning it.

"In fact, I guess I'd better sign your book before I forget about it." Stephanie turned toward the rear seat where the shopping bags had been placed.

"Forget about it?" Molly teased. "Some best friend!"

Stephanie reached and got the poetry book.

"Write in it while I'm driving and it'll be all scribbly," Molly fussed.

"Don't worry," Stephanie said, looking for a pen in her purse, "I only have to write six words."

"Six words? That's all?" Molly contemplated for a moment. "To Molly, from Stephanie, Happy Birthday. That's six words."

Stephanie grinned. "I wasn't counting those words."

"Oh, so you'll write those six words plus six other words?"

Nodding, Stephanie laughed. "Something like that!" She found a pen and opened the front cover of the book. "Just miss the pot-holes while I'm composing."

"Composing?" Molly huffed. "It hardly sounds like you're planning to write a sonnet, Steph!"

Stephanie rested the book on her lap and began writing.

"There's a curve coming, so don't mess up!" Molly said.

Raising her head, Stephanie watched the road, then shifted her weight and went back to her task.

"I'm done!" Stephanie shut the book.

"So fast?" Molly exclaimed. "You hardly wrote a thing! Read it to me!"

Stephanie twisted around and gently tossed the book and her purse onto the backseat.

"Hey!" Molly groused. "I wanna hear it!"

Stephanie chuckled. "Can't you wait for anything?"

"Nope." Molly looked at Stephanie and gave her a silly grin.

"OK," Stephanie conceded, watching the road. "To Molly, Happy Birthday. Our friendship has been my privilege. Love, Steph."

Molly's smile grew lovelier. "That's nice. Thank you."

Stephanie leaned back in her seat, again closing her eyes. She let out a sigh. "Twelve words, just in case you're counting."

"I was."

Both of them laughed, feeling better about things.

CHAPTER NINETEEN

Help

James's eyes fed on the last section of Scripture that Molly had assigned to him: "Who shall separate us from the love of Christ? Shall trouble or hardship or persecution or famine or nakedness or danger or sword? . . . For I am convinced that neither death nor life, neither angels nor demons, neither the present nor the future, nor any powers, neither height nor depth, nor anything else in all creation, will be able to separate us from the love of God that is in Christ Jesus our Lord."

As the magnitude of the words hit him, James slumped back in his chair. He wondered whether these verses had been included in his junior high Sunday school lessons, since the focus was love.

"Trouble, hardship, persecution, danger, and sword," he grumbled, naming his own adversities. He pondered each one, deciding they had collectively removed him from love. *But whose love? The love of God? Of people? Of self?*

His eyes raced over the page again. ". . . that neither the present nor the future . . . nor anything else . . . will be able to separate us from the love of God." The words rolled off his tongue, and he felt suddenly convicted. He knew he had given the past twenty-eight years over to separation from almost everything he previously had held dear. At age twenty-three, he'd pulled the plug, deep-sixing his future, hating his present, and aching for his past.

Should he take the blame? Wasn't it a "sword"—a bomb— that had detached his body from his life? Wasn't it trouble and the death of a friend that had revealed how much the Lord really loathed him? Or was it, in fact, that he had utterly despised himself?

"God, help me," he muttered, throwing back his head and glimpsing upward. He half-expected an angel, or maybe a divine aura at least. Instead, he saw a white ceiling with a long spackle mark where a crack had been filled.

"Help," he pleaded again.

For a moment, nothing came to him. Then a vision appeared, not on the ceiling, but in his mind's eye. A face. Not clear, yet clear enough.

"Wayne," he said. Then, like a bubble bursting, the image disappeared, leaving James marvelling.

He remembered his last visit to Wayne's Market, the horrible flashback, and Wayne's invitation to get together. The man's smile had been warm, and he had delighted in the discovery of a fellow veteran.

Why him? James thought, getting up and letting Kelly back into the house. The dog appeared overheated, her tongue lolling out. She headed straight to her water dish in the kitchen.

"Been chasing the squirrels?" James called after her with a chuckle. He looked at his watch. It was just after 5 P.M. Perhaps he still had time to "chase" after the meaning of his "vision"—Wayne Summers.

"Wanna go to town, Kelly?" He heard her lapping at the bowl, then she came to him with tail wagging and water dripping off her chin.

Two minutes later, they were in the truck and on their way to Coeur d'Alene. James laughed at his impulsiveness, recognizing he had never gone to the city twice in one week before, let alone twice in one day. In fact, he didn't have a clue as to the purpose of this trip; he only hoped Wayne would provide an answer.

"Got to find out!" he told himself, feeling unusually buoyant. He noted that Kelly was standing up and looking feisty, contrary to her normal sprawl. She obviously sensed the excitement.

"You're wondering what's gotten into me, hey, Kelly?" He patted her head, pondering the question. Quickly, he determined that something had indeed "gotten into" him. Whether it was God or hope, folly or dementia, he wasn't sure. But he had revelation and unexpected courage going for him at the moment, and he rode the swell into downtown Coeur d'Alene.

After parking in front of the grocery, James left Kelly in the truck and headed for the main entrance. With every step he took, though, he felt his confidence waning. By the time he saw Wayne Summers, he wasn't sure he could follow through.

Wayne, coming up an aisle from the back of the store, offered a sunny smile, giving James hope.

"Hi, Jon! How are ya?"

"Good," James said nervously, and they shook hands. "I'd like to talk with you, um, if you've got time."

"Absolutely! In fact, I was gonna take a break in the back. Follow me!"

Wayne led the way to a storage room laden with boxes, many of which were empty. A table and two folding chairs were crammed into a corner, and a nearly drained coffeepot sat on an upended wooden crate.

"Can I get you some coffee?" Wayne asked, gesturing for James to sit down.

"No, thanks."

Both of them took a seat.

"Good thing. The coffee's been there all day." Wayne chuckled and gave James's shoulder a slap.

James tried futilely to form a grin. "Ah, by the way, my name is James. James Wade."

Wayne cocked a thick eyebrow. "Oh, I'm sorry. I've been calling you Jon."

"That's OK, my pen name's Jon. Jonathan Roseland."

"Your pen name?"

Embarrassed, James said, "Well, I've written a book—"

"A book? About the war?"

"No, poetry. I write . . . poems."

"No kidding?"

James wondered if Wayne would laugh at him.

"That's amazing," Wayne said. "I'm impressed. I've got a poet shopping at my store."

James felt encouraged, enabling him to breathe easier.

"Well, James, what'd you want to talk about?"

James hadn't thought about where to begin. He decided to simply leap in with, "How awful do I look to you?"

Startled, Wayne asked, "What do you mean?"

"Am I too repulsive to be out in public?"

Frowning, Wayne said, "Are you kiddin'? Lots of people are injured or crippled. I've got a couple of double amputees who buy groceries here."

James took off his hat and wig. "How 'bout now? Could you live with this?"

Before Wayne could open his mouth, James removed his artificial ear. "And now?"

Wayne refused to look away, even as tears filled his eyes.

Assuming he was being pitied, James disgustedly dropped the ear on the table.

"I'm not feeling sorry for you, if that's what you think," Wayne said softly. "Your scars are beautiful to me, and I mean *beautiful*."

The words had a powerful effect, piercing James's heart. He felt his own eyes welling up.

"You earned those scars, and I respect that. Our country owes you a debt of gratitude." Wayne wiped his cheeks. "Guys like us can cover up our scars if we choose to, and most of us do, but that doesn't mean we shouldn't be proud of 'em."

James's eyes opened wider. "Guys like us?"

Wayne flashed a grin, then slid his chair back and raised up his right pant leg.

"Look at this," he said, rapping his knuckles against his lower leg.

"Plastic," James replied.

Then Wayne pulled his shirttail out of his pants and twisted sideways in his seat, exposing his lower back. James saw scar tissue the size of a half dollar.

"Bullet or shrapnel?" James asked.

"Shrapnel," Wayne said, tucking in his shirt.

James sighed. "I didn't know. I never saw you limp."

Wayne scooted his chair closer to the table. "I don't limp much. Besides, *you* don't look at people enough to notice those things."

"What do you mean?" James asked.

"You shy away. You avoid eye contact. How many friends you got?"

James dropped his gaze. "None," he admitted.

"That's your fault," Wayne declared.

"My fault?"

"Yeah. You never wanted to talk before. I would've been your friend."

James made himself look up.

Grinning, Wayne said, "Get one or two more like me and you got yourself a clique!"

James tried to force a sliver of a smile, to no avail. "I lost my best friend in 'Nam," he uttered.

"Me too," Wayne said, getting serious. "I lost two friends, and it killed me for a while. But life goes on for the living, even the wounded and the crippled." He leaned closer to James, peering at him. "We didn't choose our wounds and scars. I took it in the leg and back; you got it in the face. Now we gotta make the best of it."

"But why do people have to stare?"

Wayne shrugged. "People are people. Sure, they're gonna look. They're gonna wonder what happened to you."

"Some of them run away from me," James lamented.

"That's just some. Then there's people like me, people who

would be glad to get to know you. Come by anytime. I've got a small Cessna airplane, and I fly it everywhere. I'll take you up sometime, OK?"

James studied Wayne's face, searching for phoniness. He received a genuine smile.

"I think maybe God sent me here today," James announced, picking up his artificial ear.

Wayne raised his eyebrows and widened his grin. "God did? How?"

"You won't believe it." Fingering the steel knob on the side of his head, James fastened the ear in place.

"You might be surprised," Wayne cautioned.

CHAPTER TWENTY

Wishing

Molly, now in the passenger seat, held the poetry book in her hands as Stephanie drove the car past the Stevensville turnoff toward Victor. Darkness was falling, but enough light remained for Molly to reread the dedication page.

"Dedicated to a long lost love—if only I could love a second time," Molly recited.

"Hey, that proves it!" Stephanie exclaimed.

"Proves what?"

"James has no other woman. He wrote the book for you."

Molly absorbed the dedication, realizing the truth of Stephanie's words.

"He wishes he could love you a second time," Stephanie said.

"It's not that explicit," Molly contended. "He dedicated it to me, but he says he wishes he could love a second time. It doesn't say whom. It just says he wants to love again."

Stephanie guffawed. "Come on, Moll! He still loves you!"

Shaking her head, Molly said, "You don't know that. He told me to forget about him."

"Sure, he did. He knows he hurt you, and he's insecure. Until you can forgive him, he'll keep running away."

Molly closed the book and set it on her lap. "I don't know if I can forgive him."

"You can," Stephanie stated matter-of-factly.

"What makes you think so?"

"Listen, Moll. You gave James your heart when you were young, and you never took it back. You never gave it to anyone else 'cause James owned it, even when you thought he was gone.

Now he's back, and that means, as funny as it sounds, your heart's back." Stephanie looked at Molly. "You'll be able to forgive, and maybe even love again."

Molly drummed her fingers on the book as Stephanie braked the car for a dog trotting along the shoulder of the highway.

After a moment's thought, Molly grumbled, "That's the most absurd mumbo jumbo I've ever heard."

Stephanie cracked up. "Maybe so, but I was hoping you'd buy into it!"

Molly joined in the laughter. "Yeah, right!"

As the car crested a hill, the women saw distant flames in the dusky sky.

"The moment of truth," Molly muttered. "The fire's still burning."

"I wonder how close it is to your house," Stephanie said.

"I don't know, but we'll find out in a few minutes." Molly smoothed the flat of her hand over the book cover, searching for inner strength.

Three hours earlier, the Gash Peak fire, with flames reaching nearly two hundred feet high, had jumped the line east of Glen Lake and ravaged its way another mile toward Smith Creek Drainage. At nightfall, though, as winds decreased and the air temperature cooled, the fire grew sleepy and its progress slowed. Tired fire-fighters, covered in dust and soot, watched the fire burn orange and red from a logging road a couple hundred yards to the south, eating sandwiches while waiting for a Forest Service bus to pick them up. Many of them figured that the next line would be dug on a ridge close to homes just two miles away in an effort to save property. They also knew that strong winds and low humidity were predicted for tomorrow afternoon, making for a bad day.

The helicopter and slurry bomber pilots, having been chased off the fire early in the battle, had readied seven aircrafts for a predawn strike, including six helicopters and a P-3 air tanker capable of dropping three thousand gallons of chemical fire retardant at once. The pilots wanted revenge on the inferno that had nearly snatched a Sky Crane from the air when smoke exploded from the forest, causing zero visibility for the pilot who bravely had dumped two thousand gallons of water on the sea of flames. In the smoke-out, the helicopter nearly turned on its side and just missed striking a hillside. "Now," the pilots avowed, "it's time for payback!"

Stephanie and Molly found Deputy Casman sitting in the dark in his patrol car at the end of Sweathouse Creek Road and the White's Lane turnoff. Stephanie stopped the Volvo beside the officer and rolled down her window.

"I was just at your house, Molly, for the fourth time," Cliff said, squinting his eyes.

"We had some serious business in Coeur d'Alene," Molly explained, leaning forward in her seat to look past Stephanie.

Cliff used his thumb to point over his left shoulder. "There's some serious business back there too. The fire's just two miles from your house, and we're in a Stage 3."

"Meaning?" Stephanie asked.

"That's a request for residents to leave their homes and check in at the evacuation center in the high school gym."

"When? Now?" Molly fussed, glaring at the deputy's dimly lit face.

"You've got until noon tomorrow, thanks to a calm night," Cliff said, a touch of relief in his voice. "A couple of your neighbors have left already, but most'll be packin' up early in the mornin'."

Molly shook her head. "You said the fire's still two miles away!"

Cliff nodded. "Yeah, but it's only a mile from the drainage. That's why it's dangerous."

"So, what if I don't want to leave?"

Wide-eyed, Stephanie turned toward Molly as if she had asked the most ludicrous question ever posed by humankind.

Molly met her gaze. "I'm just asking, OK? Isn't there something we could be doing to protect the house, Cliff, instead of just running away?"

"There's some stuff you can do," Cliff said, "like thinnin' brush, trimmin' branches, mowin' dry grasses, and settin' up sprinklers; that kinda stuff. You got a generator?"

"What for?" Molly asked.

"To run your sprinklers. You don't wanna leave the electricity on if the fire's gonna hit your house."

Molly shook her head. "I don't have a generator."

Cliff pursed his lips, then grinned only slightly. "Well, if you're insistent about staying. I think you should go, but I've got an old generator I don't give a hoot about, anyway. I'll drop it off early in the mornin'."

"Thanks, Cliff. I'm grateful."

"No problem. Another thing you can do is paint your house number real big on your driveway with orange paint."

"Why?"

"So the choppers can identify your place from the sky. It could help in an emergency."

"That's what I'll do!" Molly declared. "A big 2839."

"There's also an Evacuation Refusal form I'll need you to fill out if you're not outta here by noon," Cliff advised. "I'll be knockin' on everyone's doors before then."

"I thought you told me yesterday that Stage 4, not Stage 3, means mandatory evacuation," Molly quibbled.

"That's right," said Cliff, "and you can bet your bottom buck, the way things are goin', we'll be at Stage 4 by sometime tomorrow mornin'!"

Stephanie parked the Volvo in the driveway next to the old blue Ford Escort, and the women got out with their purses and purchases. They stood silently in the darkness for half a minute, watching the orange glow on the mountain beyond Molly's property. Then they entered the house through the back door and set their goods on the kitchen table.

"I know we need to pack some things," Stephanie said, "but why don't we have a piece of cake while it's still your birthday?"

"OK, but just a small piece for me," Molly replied.

Stephanie opened the cake box, revealing a chocolate cake decorated with "Happy Birthday, Molly" on top.

"First, I've got to stick forty-nine candles in it," Stephanie said with a gleam in her eye. "Go do something and I'll call you when it's ready."

"Actually, I do have something I need to do. I need to find a poem."

"Go for it," Stephanie urged.

Molly walked to the master bedroom, opened the dresser drawer, and pulled out the pile of old poems. She carried them to a recliner in the living room, flicked on a light, and sat down.

Laying the papers on her lap, she shuffled through them, stopping in the middle to read a poem dated February 3, 1971.

> Juice from an orange sun
> spills on my back,
> warming me,
> touching me
> in a wasteland
> where warmth's been shot down.
> Passion's beside me,
> not to love
> but destroy.
> Hatred swarms
> as mosquitoes cloud.
> From millions of miles,
> forever and ever—
> . . . in spite of war—
> the warm kiss comes,
> out of the blue,
> an unimpeded arrow.
> But thousands between us,

comparatively few—
. . . because of war—
perch obstacle-ridden,
rocked and treed
and watered deep,
mined and spiked
for death so cold.
A hundred paces
to nearest foes,
vipers, crocs,
and hot-barreled rifles,
all breaking hearts
the very last time.
Yet my heart's AWOL,
safe in your care,
grand in your consciousness,
granted to you.
Seeking your warmth
until I abandon
a heartless encounter
where warmth's been shot down.

Molly dropped the poem to her lap and exhaled. She remembered James's memorial service and the minister telling her the grief would gradually subside.

"He's not totally gone," she had told him, " 'cause I have his heart. It was granted to me in a letter."

Molly looked again at the old poem, which had served as the deed.

"Granted to you," she whispered, recalling her follow-up letter in which she had used the same words to give her heart to James. *Maybe Stephanie's right. I've got James's heart, and he's got mine. We just need to take them out of storage.* She shook her head and smiled at her off-the-wall analysis.

"I'm ready for you!" Stephanie called.

Molly set the poems on the floor beside her chair before getting up and going to the kitchen. She was greeted with a glowing cake and a speedy rendition of "Happy Birthday to You."

"Is that a cake disguised as a wildfire?" Molly teased.

Stephanie snickered. "Better hurry; make a wish and blow 'em out before the house burns down."

Molly made a face at her friend. "Very funny. OK, I wish . . ." She closed her eyes, tipped back her head, and drew a long breath. Then she leaned over the cake and blew away the fire.

"Good job!" Stephanie said, clapping. "What'd you wish for?"

"Can't tell or I won't get it." Molly fanned away the smoke with her hand.

Stephanie brooded for a moment. "You probably wished things could be the way they used to be between you and James."

Molly picked up a knife from the table and cut into the cake. "That would be a wasted wish," she said, lifting a slice of cake onto a plate.

"Why?"

"Because we're not in our twenties anymore, and we can't go back."

"That's true," Stephanie conceded as she sat down, "but let's talk about love. The love between you is what I'm wishing could be the same."

Molly cut another piece of cake. "A wish can't make that happen either, Steph."

Stephanie smiled. "OK, Moll, then let's not wish. Let's *pray for a miracle!*"

CHAPTER TWENTY-ONE

Holding On

James lay in the dark, listening to Kelly's loud breathing as she slept on the floor beside his bed.

While mulling over his conversation with Wayne Summers, James focused on Wayne's religious beliefs. Wayne had not been too surprised about James's vision, saying, "Where else would God send you but to a Christian?" Then Wayne shared his conversion experience, citing Romans 12:1 as the verse that had enabled him to accept his impairment.

"I urge you, brothers, in view of God's mercy, to offer your bodies as living sacrifices, holy and pleasing to God—this is your spiritual act of worship." James whispered the verse for the umpteenth time, having memorized it at his desk after getting home.

Wayne himself had done what the Scripture asked of him. He had fallen to his knees and said to the heavens, "I dedicate my body to you, Lord. Imperfect though it is, it's yours." This surrender had healed him, he said, releasing him from anger, insecurity, and fear. He was now able to live life to the fullest, secure in God's care.

James found Wayne's perspective hard to understand. His own outlook was far darker. He believed himself to be beyond healing, to which Wayne replied, "You can't get there alone, but you can get there with God."

James moved to the edge of his bed. He reached down and touched Kelly's back, causing her to stir and quit breathing so heavily. He thought about how old she was getting, realizing she'd turn thirteen in a few months.

A *teenager,* he mused, but after doing some quick multiplication, he said quietly, "Ninety-one in dog years." Then he remembered his dad, Chuck, would be seventy-five years old in three weeks.

There had been no communication between James and Chuck for more than five years. James had sent a short letter early on and had left telephone messages twice, but Chuck had not responded. When he told his son he was through with him the day before Mary's funeral, he had meant it.

James thought about his three attempts to contact his father and wondered why he had not done more. He had let the man he loved most slip out of his life with only the feeblest resistance.

Hadn't he missed his dad? Didn't he desire to see him since Chuck had remarried and moved to Orlando? *Of course I do!* he told himself, but he'd protected his heart from getting broken again by simply doing nothing. He took no risks, and without risks, there was no love.

"Fear has locked up my heart," he grumbled, kicking off the sheet and slapping his feet to the floor. Kelly flinched as James put on his terry cloth robe and brushed past her, but she didn't get up.

James turned on some lights as he made his way to his desk, then he sat down and stared at his phone. He wanted to call his dad, but he didn't know the number and suddenly lost his nerve.

"Maybe tomorrow," he muttered. Then the phone rang, making him jump. He fumbled with the receiver after a second ring, getting it to his ear.

"May I speak to James Wade?" a voice asked.

"Uh, this is he."

"Hello, Mr. Wade. My name is Jason, and I'm calling on behalf of America's Disabled Veterans. How are you this evening?"

James glanced at the wall clock. It was 9:45.

"Kinda late, isn't it?" he protested.

"I'm sorry, Mr. Wade. If this is an inconvenient time, may I call back another day?"

"Well, I am . . . a disabled veteran."

"Oh, you are?" A shuffling of papers could be heard. "Well, sir, I want you to know it's people like you we're trying to help."

James cringed at the "people like you" reference. "That's not in your script, is it? People like you?"

"Uh, no, not exactly."

"Maybe you shouldn't use a phrase like that."

"Um, I hope you have a very nice evening, Mr. Wade. Sorry for the inconvenience."

Before James could say another word, the line went dead. James hung up and sat back in his chair.

It's people like that who make people like me withdraw from society, James concluded. But instead of the dejection that usually came with such a thought, James felt something else. He felt OK. Refreshingly unperturbed.

He looked at his phone again. Boldly, he picked it up and called an operator. A minute later he had his father's new phone number, which he quickly dialed.

"Hello?" a woman's soft voice greeted him.

"Hello, um, is this the Wade residence?" James asked, acutely aware of his lisp.

"Yes, it is. May I help you?"

"This is James Wade, and . . . is my father there?"

There was momentary silence, then the woman said, "James, I'm Margaret. I've heard a lot about you."

James swallowed hard. "Probably hasn't been too good, has it?"

Margaret laughed nervously. "Better than you think, I'm sure. I'm glad you're calling."

"Thank you. Is my father—"

"Yes, I'll get him." She covered the mouthpiece, though not well enough to prevent James from hearing most of the exchange between her and Chuck. By the time she addressed James again, he already knew the verdict.

"He doesn't want to talk to me," James acknowledged sadly.

"Not right now," Margaret concurred. Then in a hushed voice she said, "But he will, James. Trust me, he will."

"You think so?"

"Yes. Give me your number."

James told her his phone number. "I guess I won't hold my breath," he joked, laughing stiffly.

"Perhaps not," Margaret replied, "but do hold on."

"Hold on?"

"Don't lose hope."

James liked this woman. "Nice talking with you, Margaret. Thanks for helping me."

"You're welcome. I'm glad you called."

"Before you go," James hurriedly asked, "is my dad doing OK?"

He could almost hear her smile.

"He's fine. Very healthy."

"Great. Um, OK, then, good-bye." He hung up, put his hands to his face, and cried. Just hearing his dad's voice, albeit muffled and stern, had melted his heart.

Kelly, drawn by her master's sobbing, nudged James's leg with her nose. James wiped his tears, leaned over, and hugged the dog's neck.

"I'm OK," he told her, and she lay at his feet.

James put his head down on the desk, feeling drained. So much had happened so quickly, yet everything remained unresolved. His future with Molly, his father, God, even Wayne—all up in the air. And all but his father were expecting further contact.

They're in a waiting room, looking for me to get my act together. But I haven't had it together for twenty-eight years, so what hope have I now?

He lifted his head and looked at the small Bible that Molly had given him. Her words spoken in front of the restaurant echoed in his mind: "You're touching the pure and lovely things of God, and you don't even know it."

Am I? he wondered. He moved his hand along the desktop until his fingers touched the soft cover of the Bible.

"Lord," he whispered, "is it possible for me to give you my bad eye, my bad ear, my rigid lips, my bum leg? To offer my beat-up body as a living sacrifice? And you'd be pleased?"

He held his breath, longing for an answer, but the room was still. He exhaled, hearing the sound linger in the air. Then he heard the faint howl of a coyote, followed by a second coyote's response.

"That's what I need," he resolved. "Feedback."

He stood up, flicked off the light, and hobbled to his bedroom—trailed by his silent, but faithful, dog.

CHAPTER TWENTY-TWO

Have's and Have-Not's

Just after the crack of dawn the next day, Cupid popped his head out of his sleeping bag and looked around the shadowy west edge of the cemetery. Stealthily in the night, he had spread a small tarp beside a tree and between two tall grave markers before unrolling his sleeping bag and crawling inside.

Spotting no one in the morning mist, he knew he had another couple of hours before the caretakers arrived. He decided to go back to sleep, trusting his inner clock to wake him.

Two hours later, he felt a tug on the sleeping bag, then a light kick to his backside.

"Huh?" he squawked, sitting up. He peered into the sun at the hulking figure of a Coeur d'Alene police officer standing over him.

"Time to move, Cupid."

"That you, Jerry?"

"Yeah, get up and get movin'."

Cupid unzipped his sleeping bag and climbed to his feet, making peace with a wide grin. "My bag's kinda damp," he said timidly.

"Roll it up anyway," the grizzled policeman ordered. "You know you're not supposed to spend the night here."

Cupid dropped to his knees, wiped some of the dew off the bag, and began rolling it up. "Where am I s'posed to be, Jerry?"

"Not here."

"But where, then?" Cupid persisted, looking at the officer's frowning face.

"Go where the other bums go, outta town somewhere."

Cupid tied off his bag and rolled up the tarp, which was wet on the underside. "So, you think I'm a bum?" he asked, stuffing the tarp into his backpack.

Jerry shrugged his big shoulders. "Seems like it. I don't know. What do you think?"

Standing up, Cupid replied, "I'm a regular guy. Just happens I don't have a job or a home right now. Got a job for me? I'll gladly work it. Windows at the police station need washin'?"

Jerry shook his head. "Just move along, that's all."

Cupid slung his pack on his shoulder and scooped up his sleeping bag. "Why is it that the have's always look down on the have-not's?"

"Start walkin' before I arrest you for loitering and violating city ordinances," Jerry warned, pointing toward the cemetery's rear exit.

Chuckling as he strolled away, Cupid said, "Just tryin' to cheer you up!"

"Doesn't sound like cheerin' up to me."

"Well," Cupid relayed over his shoulder, "it cheered me up, anyway! Have a good day, Officer Blair!" He waved and made a beeline for the street, knowing Old Jerry Blair's bark was worse than his bite. After all, the officer had threatened Cupid with arrest at least a hundred times over the years, but he'd never taken him to jail. The two of them simply played an age-old game, with one bending the rules and the other enforcing them.

As Cupid walked into town, his stomach pains reminded him that he hadn't eaten much of anything in the past twenty-four hours. Fortunately, he knew where to go to get some free food.

While Stephanie took a phone call from her husband in the kitchen, Molly sat fully dressed in the living room at eight o'clock in the morning, reading more of James's old poems. After having read them countless times while believing James was dead, a strange feeling engulfed her this time, knowing he was alive and living just four hours away. The usual image in her mind of the handsome twenty-three-year-old husband-to-be dissolved into a middle-aged marred face. The face, like James's hoax, concealed the past. Yet the eyes—even the droopy one—still glimmered with a trace of vivacity that Molly had always admired.

I wish he'd been more positive yesterday, Molly thought. She looked at the last of the forty-nine poems. It was dated May 11, 1971.

> One more poem makes 50;
>   so this is 49.
> One more day makes 300;
>   so this is 299.
> One more kiss makes 50,000;
>   so this is 49,999.
> One more thought makes a million;
>   so this is 999,999.
>
> Will you still love me at 50?
>   Will you be there tomorrow?
> Will you kiss me year after year?
>   Will you dream of me forever?
>
> Your diamond ring says
>   "Yes, indeed!"
> An eternal pledge
>   of never-ending love
> wrapped around your finger.

Molly sighed. *I never got the fiftieth poem, another day, or another kiss. Not for more than twenty-eight years.*

She got up from her chair and carried the stack of poems to her bedroom. She set the poems on the bed, then opened her drawer of treasures. She dug around until she found a tiny black jewelry box. She opened it and stared at the quarter-carat marquise diamond engagement ring.

I haven't worn this for years, she thought, taking the ring out of the box. She slipped it halfway onto her ring finger, but purposely stopped at the middle knuckle.

I won't put it on without rekindled love. She admired the diamond for a moment before taking off the ring and putting it on the bed beside the poems, intending to gather up everything within the hour.

"Phil can't believe all that's happening," Stephanie told Molly as they met in the kitchen.

"Did you tell him we can't believe it either?" Molly asked.

"Ouch!" Stephanie clutched at her lower back, grimacing.

"You OK?"

Stephanie forced a smile. "Just a twinge," she said, rubbing the spot.

Molly shook her head. "So, Phil was right about your water-skiing injury. All that packing we did last night wasn't good for it."

"It won't stop me from helping more this morning," Stephanie insisted.

"Yeah," Molly mumbled, "the fire." She glanced out the kitchen window and saw movement on the ridge less than a hundred yards from her house. Looking closer, she counted four bulldozers and at least a dozen firefighters.

"They're digging a big trench," she told Stephanie, who joined her at the window. The two women saw smoke rising from the top of the mountain more than a mile away as a helicopter flew in to make a water drop.

"Look right here!" Stephanie said, pointing at two firefighters who had suddenly appeared around the corner of the house.

A knock at the front door drew the women's attention.

"It may be Cliff," Molly said, heading toward the door. She skirted past the pile of folded clothes and four boxes that she and Stephanie had packed the previous night. Opening the door, she encountered a young, strapping male firefighter, unshaven and dressed in a soot-sodden yellow Nomex shirt, green pants, and a red hard hat.

"Good mornin', ma'am," he said with a friendly grin. "We're here to save your house."

Molly had to chuckle. "You don't say? How do you propose to do that?" She glanced over his shoulder at another helicopter advancing from the east.

"I've got a crew of twenty ready to cut brush and whack some trees. We'll remove flammables from around your property, set up a sprinkler system, and try to stop a ground fire. And we'd like to gel your house."

"Gel my house?"

The firefighter had a gleam in his blue eyes. "We'll douse the place with fire-protection chemicals. It'll cost you several hundred dollars, but I'm makin' the offer."

"Is it really necessary?" Molly asked.

"We think the fire's gonna run down the drainage and right up to that firebreak our dozer boys are diggin'. Maybe the line'll hold, and maybe it won't. But the afternoon winds are gonna be high, if the weatherman's right. If I were you, I'd go with the gel."

"Well, OK, I guess. When do you do it?"

"We'll get an engine crew in here after you evacuate, and we'll spray the whole house." He looked inside and saw a couple of boxes. "Are you ready to leave?"

"Not till the fire gets a lot closer than it is now. I'm still planning on getting out some furniture."

"Got a truck?"

"No, just those two cars in the driveway."

"Well, as you can see, there's a couple of trucks packin' my crew comin' up your driveway. While we're here workin', I'll have a couple guys help you throw a couch or two on the flatbed. No problem." He swiped his hand at pieces of ash floating in the air. "But we don't have a lot of time for movin'. There's other things to do, and I didn't rent no Ryder truck, ma'am."

CHAPTER TWENTY-THREE

Finding Help

James sat on his front porch in the cool morning air, eating a bagel. Chummy had scampered to within ten feet of him, watching his every move.

Taking another bite, James chewed loudly before saying, "Mmm, that's good, Chummy. Want some?" He tore off a piece and flipped it halfway to the squirrel. With little hesitation, Chummy darted forward and clutched the bread with his front claws. The squirrel sat on his haunches and nibbled away, five feet from James.

Farther out, James saw Edgy moving in. *Let's see if I can get him closer.* He chomped on the bagel and made tantalizing, slurping noises. Edgy responded by scurrying to within eight or nine yards, where he paused and twitched as though his tail had found a light socket.

James pinched off a chunk of bagel and threw it toward Edgy, causing Chummy to jump. The toss went about fifteen feet.

"Come on," James coaxed. "Let's be pals." Edgy skittered forward, finding the bagel a split second before Chummy did. Snatching it in his mouth, Edgy spun around and retreated up a tree with his prize.

He reminds me of me, James thought. *I'm always running away. Running from everything, everybody, God . . . especially from myself. Can I change now?* He tossed another wad of bagel at Chummy and ate the remaining portion himself. Then he stood up and went into the house, finding Kelly curled up on the floor next to his desk. She seemed to grin at him as he sat down.

James rested his elbows on his desk and put his chin in his

hands. *Edgy came closer than ever today, making progress like I need to do. If not now, it may never happen. This is my chance.*

He took a piece of paper out of the desk drawer and inserted it into his typewriter. He pondered for a while, then began to type. Fifteen minutes later, he stared at his composition.

> There's a little piece of the kingdom
>   hidden away in my heart;
> I know it's a force
>   to keep me on course,
>   for without it I can't be a part.
> A part of that celestial kingdom
>   locked safely away in my soul;
> A light that one day
>   will show me the way
>   to everything I need to be whole.
> A little piece of the kingdom,
>   made of iron, not clay;
> A little piece of the kingdom
>   inside me to guide me
>   the rest of the way.

James was amazed. He knew he had touched something spiritual, and he wondered how he had done it. *Maybe God did it,* he thought.

Opening the top drawer of his desk, James took out a small, round mirror and looked at his face. For almost a minute, he stared without making his usual groaning sounds. Instead, he studied every defect and crinkle.

"So God," he said quietly, "can you use a watery eye and petrified lips?" A sense of anxiety flooded him, and he knew he had to do something, go somewhere, talk to someone—so unlike his normal self.

Maybe it's time to go back to church, he thought, *but it's Friday. Still, maybe a pastor's working in his office.*

James pushed his chair away from the desk and looked at his

dog. "How about another road trip, Kelly?" he asked, baffled by his own suggestion.

Thirty minutes later, James spotted a church. The front door was invitingly propped open, and James reacted with a quick swerve into a parking space. He turned off the truck engine and read the sign on the lawn: Coeur d'Alene Faith Fellowship, Where God Impacts Lives.

There must be someone here who can help me, James thought. He reached out and petted Kelly, who was standing on the seat and seemingly wondering what her master was going to do. But James didn't do anything for a couple of minutes. He stared blankly at the church door, wishing for a revelation.

Suddenly a tall, straggly-looking fellow appeared in the doorway. He stepped onto the concrete porch, grinning and waving at the sky as he looked up at an elm tree filled with sparrows. He set a bedroll and brown grocery bag on the porch, took off his backpack and unzipped the top.

What on earth? James thought as the man began tossing handfuls of birdseed onto the lawn beneath the tree. *Cupid?*

"I'll be right back, Kelly," James said, grabbing his cane and sliding out of the truck. He slammed the door and started toward the vagrant, who had looked his way.

Cupid, his face lighting up, watched James come. He had recognized the poet right off—cowboy hat, wig, and all.

"Jonathan Roseland! I got a copy of your book!" Cupid called out as James approached. "Lemme cheer you up!"

James's eyes brightened. "That's what I need." He shook Cupid's outstretched, grimy hand.

"Take a load off, my man," Cupid said, pointing at the porch. "Let's watch the birdies eat." He sat down on the top step and reached into the brown bag. "The Reverend came through with some rolls and breakfast bars, so we can eat too. I call it 'manna from the manse.' He's a good Reverend." Cupid took a breakfast bar from the bag and handed it to James.

"You'd better keep it for yourself," James said as he sat down.

Cupid brushed off the suggestion. "Don't worry 'bout it. There's plenty more where that came from. They got a thing here called Granny's Cupboard, and I'm pretty much Granny." He crowed and slapped his thigh.

James laughed.

"So," asked Cupid, "what you up to?"

"Looking for some answers," James said, tearing off the wrapper and taking a bite of the breakfast bar.

"Church ain't a bad place to look," Cupid said. He took a roll out of the bag. "And even if I do say so, I'm kind of an answer man, myself."

"That right?" James said, giving Cupid a sideways glance.

"Yep, so my friends all tell me." Cupid bit into the roll with a twinkle in his eye. He chewed a moment, then said, "How 'bout your wife? Couldn't she help you with some answers?"

"She's not my wife."

"Huh?"

"That woman you thought was my wife? She's not."

"You don't say?" Cupid frowned and became solemn. "Well, sir, I was married for a good bunch o' years, and I know one thing for sure."

James looked at Cupid, waiting for the answer.

"If you love 'em, you gotta tell 'em," Cupid declared. "Don't hold it back. Women don't want you to hold it back."

"Hold it back?" James asked. "Love?"

"*Tellin'* 'em! Don't hold back *tellin'* 'em," Cupid said, flashing his gap-toothed grin.

James watched a couple of sparrows pecking at the seed under the elm.

"Do you love that pretty woman?" Cupid asked bluntly.

James nodded. "Yes." His answer, sounding in his good ear, made his heart flutter. He had finally given voice to a truth he had muzzled for years, and his audience was a solitary man of the street. James smiled inside at the unpredictability of it.

"When was the last time you told her?" Cupid probed deeper.

James looked straight into Cupid's eyes. "Twenty-eight years ago."

Cupid jerked back with a look of horror. "Man, what's wrong with you? Cat had your tongue?"

Shaking his head, James said, "You don't understand. I hadn't seen her for twenty-eight years before yesterday."

"Oh, OK," Cupid uttered, nodding his head. "I guess that explains why you're here, and not helpin' with the fire and all."

James stopped chewing his food. "What fire?"

Cupid cocked his head. "Well, the other lady, Stephanie, said a big wildfire's comin' down a draw, and the house is in its path. I kinda thought it was your house."

Suddenly alarmed, James set the remainder of the breakfast bar beside him. "Neither one of them said a word about it to me!"

"From the sounds of it," Cupid said, "the fire's lickin' at the back door, and Stephanie was plumb worried."

James took his cane and clambered to his feet. He wanted to shout in frustration, but instead he turned his face to the blue sky and pronounced firmly, "Twenty-eight years ago, fire took her love away. I can't let it take her home." He turned a half circle. "I need a phone."

Cupid hopped to his feet. "The Rev's inside. He'll help you."

CHAPTER TWENTY-FOUR

To the Rescue

Sitting at the church secretary's desk where the pastor had led him, James took the paper with Molly's phone number from his wallet. He dialed and waited.

Stephanie answered after the third ring. "Hello?"

"Stephanie? This is James," he announced hastily. "What's going on?"

"James!" She took a moment to gather her thoughts. "Well, we're packing and, um, there are firemen here trying to save Molly's house."

"How close is the fire?"

Stephanie took a couple of steps toward the kitchen window. "I don't know," she said, looking outside. "Maybe a mile."

"A mile? That sounds far away."

"Believe me, it's not. It's at the top of a drainage full of trees and brush and . . . it's a bad situation. The wind seems to be picking up."

"Where's Molly?"

"She's outside, painting the house number on the driveway."

"What?"

"So the helicopters can see it from the air. You wanna talk to her?"

Ignoring the question, James asked one of his own. "How soon before the fire reaches the house?"

"I don't know, James. It could be a few hours, maybe less. Maybe they'll stop it, but we're supposed to be evacuated by noon."

"How can I find you?"

"Huh?" Stephanie asked.

"Where in Victor?"

"Uh, where the fire is. 2839 White's Lane. You can't miss the smoke."

"Tell Molly I'll be there!" James said.

"What?" Stephanie blurted just as the line went dead.

James looked at his watch. *Seven-thirty. Eight-thirty in Montana.* He walked out of the secretary's office and located the pastor in his study.

"Thank you," James said, reaching for his wallet. "Let me pay you for—"

"Not necessary," the pastor replied. "This one's on God."

James nodded his head. "OK, thanks. Maybe I'll see you in church sometime."

The pastor smiled. "That would be nice. God bless you."

James left the building and found Cupid still sitting on the front porch.

"You wanna help me?" James asked as he walked down the steps.

"And howdy!" Cupid said, getting up. "Whaddya need?"

"Come with me."

Cupid grabbed his backpack, bedroll, and grocery bag and followed James to his truck.

"What's the plan?" Cupid asked, tossing his belongings into the rear of the truck before opening the passenger door.

"That's Kelly," James said as the dog gave Cupid's hand a lick.

"She's a beaut," complimented Cupid, climbing in beside her.

James got in and started the engine. Driving off, he said, "We're going to Wayne's Market. Do you know Wayne Summers?"

"Yep. A nice guy."

"Wayne's got a plane," James explained. "I'm gonna ask him to fly me to Montana, to the site of the fire." James looked past Kelly at Cupid. "If Wayne can do it, I'll need you to watch my dog."

Cupid put his arm around Kelly's neck. "No problem. Will she stay with me?"

"I hope so. She's been a one-man dog all her life."

Hugging Kelly, Cupid said, "I think we'll get along just fine. I can tie a rope to her collar, though, to keep her close."

"Thanks," James said.

"I'll walk her 'round town and introduce her to all my friends," Cupid suggested, grinning. "That oughta cheer 'er up!"

James gave Cupid a concerned look. "She's not used to lots of people."

Cupid winked. "My friends are seagulls and squirrels."

"OK," James agreed, "I think Kelly will like that."

Cupid petted Kelly's head, then shrugged. "Why me?"

"Huh?"

"Why you trustin' me with your dog?"

James chuckled. "That's easy. A man who cares enough to feed the birds is a man I can count on with my dog."

"You got that right!" Cupid said, delighted.

Within an hour, James was buckled up and wearing a headset in the passenger seat of a Cessna 182 Skylane at the small Coeur d'Alene Airport located six miles north of town. He had placed his hat on the rear seat and watched Wayne Summers perform a ten-minute preflight exterior and interior examination of the red-and-white single-engine plane after procuring a full briefing from Flight Service. Then after taxiing to the hold-short line and getting cleared for takeoff, Wayne gunned the Cessna down the runway, reaching 60 knots before lifting off.

James felt the G-forces as he watched the ground seemingly drop out from beneath him.

"How you doin'?" Wayne asked.

"Good," James said, holding his stomach.

"We should be at the Hamilton, Montana, airport in an hour and ten minutes," Wayne related over the engine roar. "That'll be

11:50. There'll be a courtesy car there we can use. Victor's just ten or twelve miles north of the airport. I know the area well. It's a great place to go fishing on the Bitterroot River."

James watched as Wayne set the manifold pressure and the power setting for climb. "So the airport's south of the fire?"

"That's right," Wayne said. He retracted the flaps and adjusted the trim.

"Then to get to Hamilton, we'll have to fly over the fire? We'll get to see it from the air?"

"Yup. If it's on the west side of Highway 93, we'll fly by on the east side, and vice versa if it's on the east side, so you'll see it from a couple miles away, I'd say."

James nodded, feeling a bit jittery in the small plane. Through his headset, he heard an air traffic controller say, "8414 Tango. There's traffic bearing two-niner-zero at eight-thousand-five-hundred at two o'clock, five miles. Confirm your altitude, seven-thousand-five hundred."

"OK, this is Cessna 8414 Tango," Wayne responded. "Confirm altitude seven-thousand-five hundred. Acknowledge traffic bearing two-niner-zero, eight-thousand-five hundred at two o'clock. Scanning for traffic." He released the mike button, then looked at James. "This woman means a lot to you, doesn't she?" he asked with a friendly smile.

James took a full breath. "Everything," he confessed for the second time that day.

Wayne's grin stretched wider. "So, your scars don't matter anymore?"

"Not today," James conceded, feeling tougher. "They don't matter today."

"Glad to hear it," Wayne said. He gave the control yoke a little slap and went back to scanning the skies for traffic.

CHAPTER TWENTY-FIVE

Firestorm

When glowing embers from the Gash Peak fire ignited in the Smith Creek Drainage, the firefighters on the mountain bailed out. A microburst, or wind shear, had leveled many of the trees ten years earlier at the top of the drainage, and the downed timber had not been cleared on the steep eastern slope. Also, a dense cover of young, sappy fir with thin bark and low-sweeping branches provided abundant fuel for the blaze.

In minutes, the ravine looked like a gigantic campfire. The trees remaining from the old blowdown sent streams of flame almost two hundred feet above the fallen timber. Fire whirls erupted in ponderosa pine clusters on the fringes of the microburst, and with every gust of wind, another point of fire burst forth. In the heaviest timber, fire created its own wind, whipping trees back and forth as they went up in a blaze of glory, sending sparks spiraling high into the sky.

The bulldozer operators working on the ridge above a stretch of homes on White's Lane had dug a thirty-foot-wide line, long enough to protect all of the endangered properties from an approaching run-of-the-mill wildfire. But as the crew completed their job, the firestorm to the west was anything but ordinary. Churning down the draw was a fast-burning crown fire, leaping between treetops and throwing spot fires out to extraordinary distances. The bulldozer crews and the structure protection crews were all aware that the moment of truth was quickly coming, when their efforts would face the ultimate test.

At Molly's house, four firefighters had carried two couches, a recliner, and the dining room set to the Forest Service truck, which then moved north to the adjacent properties as the firefighters' work progressed. Molly and Stephanie had loaded some light furnishings and several boxes of belongings into both of Molly's cars, then made a final sweep of the house, stuffing their jeans pockets with jewelry and trinkets.

"It's almost noon," Stephanie said from inside the back screen door, "and that fire boss told us to leave fifteen minutes ago."

Molly was standing on the porch, sizing up the sprinkler system that the firefighters had jerry-rigged using Cliff Casman's old generator, irrigation pipes, and synthetic-coated cotton hose to wet down the lawn. She looked up at the burning mountain. With the fire just half a mile away, the trees exploded in flames, and smoke coiled upwards into a black funnel resembling a cyclone.

"Listen," Molly said. "You can hear it."

The two women stood still, mesmerized by the moment, their hearts in their throats.

"Sounds like a rushing river," Molly stated.

"It's getting scary!" Stephanie exclaimed.

Suddenly the women heard the siren go off at the downtown Victor Fire Station, even though it sounded from three miles away.

"That's the final signal for mandatory evacuation," said Stephanie. "We gotta go!" The women began walking around the side of the house.

"But what about James?" Molly asked with a groan. "He said he'd be here!"

"That's right, but it's a four-hour drive, remember?" Stephanie glanced at her watch. "He can't possibly show up for at least another hour and a half!"

Molly nodded. "OK, Steph, we'll leave. You drive the Volvo, and I'll be right behind you in the old beater."

"To the evacuation center?"

"Not right away," Molly said. "Let's drive to Sweathouse Creek Road where the roadblock and cops are. I want to see what happens from there."

Pausing beside Molly's cars, the women watched as two fire engines rolled up the driveway. The first engine was driven across the front lawn to the opposite side of the house. The driver gave the women a "thumb's up" sign. The second tanker left the driveway to park in the yard at the southeast corner of the house, nearer to Molly and Stephanie. Two firefighters climbed out of the cab while two others unrolled a fire hose from the top deck.

"We've got ten minutes to gel your house!" one of the men hollered. "It's too dangerous for longer than that! Did you turn off the electricity?"

Molly shouted, "I'll get it!" Then she said to Stephanie, "OK, get going. The keys are in the car. I'm gonna run inside and hit the main power switch."

"You'll be right behind me?" Stephanie made sure.

"Yes, don't worry." Molly turned and jogged toward the back of the house. When she disappeared around the corner, Stephanie watched the firemen turn a valve and spray a frosty, white layer of retardant onto the front roof of the house. The coating resembled the soap suds at a carwash as bubbly streams washed down the outside walls.

After wiping ash off the windshield and climbing into the Volvo, Stephanie started the car and backed down the driveway. Her eyes darted from the rearview mirror to the bustling fire crews to the blaze on the mountainside. As she swung the car onto White's Lane and braked, she focused on the old Escort parked in the driveway, expecting to see Molly at any second. She hesitated, thinking about waiting, then she saw a police car further down the road with its flashers running. She drove slowly toward the vehicle, deciding Molly would be OK with all the firefighters outside her house.

The firemen, concentrating on their task, were aware that a car had left Molly's property, but none had paid attention to the number of occupants in a vehicle stuffed with boxes, lamps, and other household items. Hence, as the house was doused with gel, the crew boss assumed that the two women were gone. Just to be sure, he fumbled with the slippery, gelled front door knob, then yelled inside the house. He received no answer.

Seconds later, the personality of the fire became even more menacing. The winds increased and grew erratic, sending flames racing down the mountain. With a sound like jet engines, the inferno exploded out both sides of the drainage in 250-foot-high walls, becoming a fire hurricane. Pine cones, sticks, and dirt spewed out of the flames.

Suddenly a big bull pine tree ignited across the bulldozer line just a hundred yards from Molly's house, then a second tree lit up. The firemen hastily reeled in their hoses, having had time to gel only three sides of the house. They drove their engines out the driveway as a clump of Bermuda grass in Molly's backyard burst into flame, despite the sprinklers. A small meadow to the south caught fire from the radiant heat. Unless a miracle occurred, the firestorm would soon hit Molly's house.

Little did Stephanie know that Molly had opened the fuse box in the kitchen pantry and received a 120-volt jolt from a wire that had shorted out on the panel door. The shock had thrown Molly backwards, and as she fell, her head hit the pantry doorjamb and knocked her unconscious. She had been left lying on the kitchen floor.

CHAPTER TWENTY-SIX

Staring Down Death

The police car hogged the middle of the road, forcing Stephanie to stop. She saw Cliff Casman driving, and as he moved the cruiser over to pull alongside her, she was shocked to see James Wade perched in the front passenger seat.

"James!" she cried, rolling down her window. "What are you doing?"

"I'm takin' him to the house!" Cliff said excitedly.

Simultaneously, James asked, "Where's Molly?"

"She's right behind me!"

Cliff and James glanced down the road, only to see two fire engines advancing out of the smoky haze.

"Where?" James demanded.

"In a blue Escort!" Stephanie scanned her rearview mirror, then stared at James in horror. "She's not coming!"

"Let's go get her!" James commanded the cop, slapping the dash.

Cliff eyed his passenger, hesitating briefly. Then he looked to the retreating fire engines and the blackened sky, and he responded to a surge of adrenalin by punching the accelerator to the floor.

"Get to safety!" Cliff yelled over his shoulder, but Stephanie did not hear him above the revved-up motor. She craned her neck and watched the police unit speed away, then she drove her own car out ahead of the firemen.

In the police car, Cliff and James sat on the edge of their seats. The closer they got to Molly's house and the raging fire, the faster their hearts pounded.

"I don't know about this!" Cliff stated, suddenly questioning the wisdom of attempting this rescue.

"It's big!" James said, sizing up the wall of fire closing in on the back of Molly's house.

The deputy slammed on the brakes just before the driveway, and the cruiser almost skidded past.

"There's her car!" He nodded toward the parked Escort.

"Let's go!" James yelled, pointing up the driveway.

Cliff cranked hard on the steering wheel to make the turn, then stopped the car. The sky over the house had become black, and a wind gust started a garbage can tumbling down the pavement.

"It's already too hot out there!" Cliff warned, losing his nerve as blowing embers showered the car's windshield. "We gotta back off!"

James jerked open his door and fell onto the driveway with his cane in hand.

"What are you doin'?" Cliff cried frantically over the deafening roar of the firestorm.

"Get outta here!" James shouted, scrambling to his feet. He limped toward the house, gritting his teeth and bucking the hot wind. His hat blew off and sailed away, but he grabbed the wig, plucked it from his head, and stuffed it inside his shirt.

Cliff, stunned by James's sudden move, shouted after him and took his foot off the brake. The car lurched forward several feet up the driveway before Cliff depressed the pedal again. In the next moment, a scorched lawn chair hurtled through the air and smashed against the front hood, then flipped up and over the roof.

"Man!" Cliff exclaimed, barely able to see James's silhouette in the smoke. He rammed the car into reverse and honked the horn twice in a last-ditch effort to get James to come back. Then his eyes focused on the house number painted in orange on the driveway.

He snatched the radio transmitter and barked, "Mayday, Mayday! Two people are trapped in a house at 2839 White's Lane! 2-8-3-9 White's Lane! Mayday!"

Meanwhile, James had made it up the slick front porch. He slipped and fell to his knees at the door, dropping his cane into the gel. Leaving the cane, he grabbed the slimy doorknob, pulled himself up, and with legs drenched in retardant, he barged into the house. He vaguely heard the police car burn rubber on the road as he shut the door behind him.

The living room, with gel on the windows, was dim, but the air was fresh and cooler. James took a deep breath as he clumped toward the kitchen.

"Molly!" he bellowed. "Molly!" Suddenly, the window above the kitchen sink, which had not been gelled, shattered. An ear-splitting rumble and rush of searing wind met James at the kitchen doorway, causing him to abruptly turn away. He headed down the hallway toward the master bedroom.

"Molly!" he cried again, stumbling into the bathroom. The big, plastic skylight above the cast iron tub made a loud, screeching noise, as it twisted and contracted from the outside heat. James sprang back as the whole thing caved in and plunged into the tub. Again, a monstrous roar and hot air poured through the hole in the ceiling, and James knew the firestorm had overtaken the house. He grabbed the shriveled plastic and heaved it out of the tub. Closing the tub drain, he turned the cold water valve all the way on. A torrent of water shot out of the faucet.

"Molly!" he screamed. He lumbered through the bedroom and back down the hallway. The shrill ring of the smoke alarm in the living room accosted him. Suffocating smoke and heat engulfed him, doubling him over at the kitchen doorway. Coughing, he wiped the tears from his stinging eyes, staggered into the kitchen, and fell in a heap on the floor. The linoleum felt warm against his hands as he rolled over and clambered to his knees.

Suddenly, a tongue of fire spit through the window over the sink, igniting the curtains and feasting on the oxygen in the room. Two explosions sounded, and James knew the tires on the Escort had blown.

Forgive me, Molly! echoed in his brain. *I'm sorry for every-thing!* He took a shallow, stifling breath, believing it to be one of his last. Then, through the rolling smoke, he saw her, lying on her back fifteen feet away.

CHAPTER TWENTY-SEVEN

Last Breaths

Wet with perspiration, James crawled on his hands and knees to Molly's limp body, coughing all the way. Her eyes were closed, but her face was flushed. He shook her and patted her cheeks.

Molly's eyes opened and she regarded James's face as he hunched over her. Disoriented, she saw two of him.

"Your house is on fire!" he shouted, pulling her by the shoulders into a sitting position.

"James?" she uttered, too softly for him to hear over the din, but he read her lips. Then she coughed and passed out once again.

James scooped Molly into his arms and struggled to his feet. Cradling her, he struggled out of the broiling kitchen to the center of the living room. The shrieking firestorm surrounded the house.

We're trapped! he thought, knowing that running outdoors would be a flight into a furnace of death. Choking on every breath, he hastened down the cloudy hallway, careening off the wall but keeping his balance with a series of small, quick steps.

"I love you, Molly!" he declared, his arm muscles burning with her weight. He saw her eyes gazing emptily at him, and for a moment he envisioned Bill Bayliss's last look when the bullet had taken his life.

Not now! James screamed inside, fearing a flashback. He tottered to the bathroom, holding Molly with his last bit of strength. In the haze and seething heat, he saw the water gushing out of the tub faucet, but he heard only the fire's raging howl.

"Hold your breath!" he cried, then he dumped Molly into the tub. Cold water splashed into his lap, and he stumbled backwards. Regaining his balance, he saw Molly flailing in the water. He yelled at her again as he stepped into the tub beside her. Frantically, he gulped some toxic air and shoved Molly under as he lay himself down. He closed his eyes as the water surged over his face. Looking up through the ripples, he saw the hole in the roof where the skylight had been. Then he saw something else—a circular whirling. A gyration. He focused on the edge of the rotation, distinguishing a helicopter blade.

It's a flashback, he told himself. He blinked his eyes, but to his amazement, the chopper was still there. His hand found Molly's, and he grasped it just as she raised up for air.

She'll burn her lungs! he thought as he pulled her back down.

Seconds later, James threw his head out of the water and inhaled. A hot pain stabbed the middle of his chest. Simultaneously, hundreds of gallons of cold water crashed through the ceiling, deluging the room. The force knocked James's head against the tub's edge, and for a moment he saw stars. Then a second wave dropped from above, washing Molly out of the overflowing tub and onto the flooded floor. She coughed and sputtered as she labored to get to her knees.

James fought his way to her side, sloshing around in foot-deep water until he made it to his feet. The air was suddenly cool and cleansed, and he gratefully filled his damaged lungs with deep breaths.

"What's happening?" Molly cried, peeling wet hair from her eyes and gasping.

"The helicopter was real!" James shouted. He heard a thunderous slap against the roof on the south side of the house. "They're dropping water!"

He waded to the window facing the backyard. "The fire's blown by!" he exclaimed, realizing the racket was diminishing.

"But the bedroom's on fire!" Molly squealed, plodding toward him. "There's no way out!"

James jerked on the window to open it, but the extreme heat had warped the wood. He pulled a wet towel from the rack, wrapped it around his right hand, and put his fist through the glass.

"This way out!" he said, punching the fragments out of the window sill.

Molly forged through the water as it flowed from the bathroom into the bedroom. James draped the towel over the bottom edge of the sill, took Molly's hand, and helped her climb out the window. Clumsily, he followed, spitting up soot, and the two of them struggled past Cliff's charred generator, across the blackened lawn, and to a green patch of grass the flames had skirted. Breathlessly, they sat down in the oasis. Everything around them smoldered.

Still coughing and gasping, they watched a Sky Crane swoop down to drop water on the house behind the three other helicopters that had flown off to refill at the Bitterroot River. A couple of hundred yards to the north, the main fire consumed the neighbor's property.

"We're alive," Molly said, looking at the sopping-wet man sitting beside her holding his knees to his chest. She took a deep breath, coughed a few more times, and leaned back on her elbows, panting for air.

"Barely," James wheezed. He slowly shook his head.

"You saved my life, James." She spoke just loud enough for him to hear over the distant roar of the firestorm.

He turned and looked into her eyes. Gasping, he said weakly, "That's the least I could do after taking away twenty-eight years of your life, isn't it?"

Finishing his water drop, the Sky Crane pilot hovered for a moment over the house, waving his hand. James expressed his gratitude with a crisp military salute, then the helicopter sailed off toward the river.

"Those guys saved us both," James said.

Molly surveyed her house. Though the fire had been doused on the outside by the helicopters, flames were visible inside the kitchen and upstairs.

"I'm gonna lose my home," she lamented, wrapping her arms

across her chest. She fought off the urge to cry, then looked at James. "How'd you get here so fast?"

James tried to smile, but coughed instead. "A friend of mine flew me in his plane," he finally answered.

"A friend?" she said, sniffling. "I thought you didn't have any friends."

"Well, I guess I've got a couple." James picked a blade of grass and rubbed it between his thumb and forefinger. He coughed again from the smoke, then cleared his throat and continued. "I'm thinking maybe God's my friend, after all."

Molly leaned closer. "Take it from me. He is."

"You can say that even as your house burns right in front of you?"

"Yes, I can. God made sure I didn't die, and he made sure you didn't either. So, praise God."

James looked up into the soupy sky. "I guess you could say he penetrated my fog."

"That was my birthday wish yesterday!" Molly revealed.

"What do you mean?"

"That God would penetrate your fog!"

James shook his head. "Oh, come on!"

"Really!" Molly reached out and briefly touched James's shoulder. "Not those exact words, but that exact meaning!"

"Well, then, I guess you got your wish."

Smiling, Molly glanced back at her house, then focused on the Escort at the top of the driveway. "Look at my car!" she blurted.

"Fried," James pronounced.

"It was packed full of my possessions! I'm trying to remember which car contained your poems." She looked hopefully at James. "I think it was the other one."

The sound of a siren reached them. Molly spied a police car traveling up White's Lane, though it was still half a mile away.

"Here comes Cliff Casman," she said. After a quick coughing fit, she added, "He's a friend of mine."

"A good friend," James replied. "He risked his life to get me here."

A fire engine appeared further down the road.

"I don't think they'll get here in time to save anything," James said solemnly.

Molly nodded her head. "At least *we* don't need saving." She reached into her pants pocket and pulled out the marquise diamond engagement ring. "But I did save this," she said, holding it up for James to admire.

He eyed the ring, then stared into Molly's eyes and said,

> "Molly, my Molly,
>   the love of my life.
> I want you forever,
>   to live as my wife.
> I offer my passion,
>   my dreams and my heart;
> a vow of a lifetime
>   till Death do us part.
> And even if Death
>   steps on stage uninvited,
> it can't touch the love
>   our two souls have united.
> Should Life smile kindly
>   for ten thousand days,
> I'll give you my love
>   in ten million ways."

Tears came to Molly's eyes. "Where'd that come from?" she asked.

"It's the last poem I wrote for you in Vietnam. I never sent it. In fact, I never really finished it, but I kept what I had in my mind."

"The fiftieth poem," Molly said softly. "Thank you." She reached out her hand. James took it, interlocking his fingers with hers.

CHAPTER TWENTY-EIGHT

Back to Life

James and Molly were taken by ambulance to the Marcus Daly Memorial Hospital in Hamilton. A pulmonologist used oxygen and a positive pressure breathing machine to counter any lung damage suffered from hot air and smoke inhalation. After a night in the ICU, both were admitted into private rooms across the hall from each other and were hooked up to oxygen tanks via long tubes and nasal cannulas.

Wayne Summers came in to wish them well, then flew his Cessna to Coeur d'Alene with a promise to check on Kelly and Cupid.

Stephanie had spent the morning and early afternoon visiting between the two hospital rooms, joking that her vacation had been ruined after all.

"Two days of sitting in a hospital is not my idea of fun," Stephanie said as she sat in a chair beside Molly's bed, "nor is staying by myself in a motel room."

Molly, unbeknownst to Stephanie, had been praying and was ready with a surprise rebuttal. "Well, I think you'll handle it OK, Steph, especially since I've decided to move to Ypsilanti for the start of school."

"No way!" Stephanie excitedly jumped to her feet.

Molly grinned. "Yes, teaching fourth grade. I might as well! The move will be a snap—one car and a tiny U-Haul trailer!"

Stephanie instantly grew serious. "Oh, Moll, you lost almost everything, and here I am rejoicing."

"Don't worry, the insurance money will put me back on my feet."

Stephanie leaned over and hugged Molly. "I don't know what

to say! I'm so glad you're coming back to Michigan, but I'm so sad you lost your house."

Squeezing Stephanie tighter, Molly said, "Everything will work itself out, I'm sure."

Stephanie sat down. "What about James?"

Molly raised her eyebrows. She glanced at her bedside table and the stack of James's old poems that Stephanie had brought to her the previous evening. "I read those forty-nine poems again," Molly said, looking back at Stephanie, "and James recited the fiftieth to me after we'd survived the fire." She licked her lips. "I know he loves me."

Stephanie nodded, sitting back. "But you're leaving here—"

"I know!" Molly laughed. "It doesn't make sense, but I need some time."

"Time for what?" James, standing in the doorway in a blue hospital gown and slippers, interrupted the conversation. He held his cane, which had survived the fire in the gel and had been delivered by Cliff Casman to the ICU. "Please excuse the attire," he said, approaching the bed. "I would've dressed up if I could have."

Stephanie arose from the chair. "Time for a late lunch!" she announced, maneuvering past James toward the door. She looked around at Molly, winked, and said, "I'll be back in an hour." Then she left the room.

"Have a seat, James," Molly offered, raising the head of her bed to the upright position.

"Did you hear the weather forecast for tomorrow?" James asked, sitting down.

"The nurse told me. Rain."

"Steady rain. Two days late."

"Yeah, after six homes were destroyed yesterday. But better late than never, I guess."

"That's what I'm here to advocate, Molly. Better late than never."

Molly understood. "I want to ask you a question, James."

"Go ahead."

"When you carried me out of my burning kitchen to the bath-tub, did I hear you say you loved me?"

James's breath caught in his throat. He swallowed, attempted a grin, and nodded.

"Why did you tell me that?" Molly asked incredulously. "You told me the day before to forget about you!"

"I've been a fool, Molly," James replied, looking askance. "All I can say is, long ago, fire took my love, my hopes, and my dreams. I let the fire steal my life." He fingered the edge of Molly's blanket. "But yesterday, when I found you and carried you down the hall-way, somehow I took everything back. When we went underwater, at first I thought I was having a flashback. But instead, I realized, at that moment, I finally gave myself, my body, to God. I told him he could take whatever's left and cut it, break it, drown it, heal it, use it—whatever he wanted—but I was his. And in those few sec-onds, something came back to me. Something was restored. A glim-mer of hope. So, I'll go from here and see what happens." He stared into Molly's brown eyes. "Maybe there's a chance . . . for us."

Molly smiled kindly. "I don't know, but I'm willing to give it some time to find out. James, I'm going back to Michigan to start over in a place where I left too many things undone. I raced out here to free myself, to find my life, but I need to go back for a while. I need to make peace with my past."

"I understand," James said softly, "because I ran away too. For too many years I've been searching for meaning, but I ended up in seclusion and misery. But now, maybe I have a chance."

"With God, you *do* have a chance!" Molly touched his hand. "And perhaps we do too. Let's start as friends."

"To be your friend is a gift," James professed.

Tears seeped into the corners of Molly's eyes. "One thing a friend must do is forgive another's mistakes." She took a breath. "I forgive you, James."

James took Molly's hand in both of his, dropped his head to the mattress, and wept. Softly, he said, "Thank you, Molly. Thank you."

Just before supper, James was sitting up in his hospital bed when his phone rang. He picked up the receiver.

"Hello?" he said.

There was nothing for a few seconds, then a deep voice said, "Hello, James?"

James's heart seemed to catch in his throat. "Dad," he blurted, "it's you!"

Again, an awkward silence fell between them.

"How did you know where to find me?" James managed to ask.

"Molly called a little while ago, and she told me about the fire," Chuck responded matter-of-factly.

"Yeah, another fire, Dad. It was terrible!" James paused for a reaction, but when none occurred, he added, "Can you believe it?"

"She said you saved her life," Chuck replied.

"We were lucky, or should I say blessed?" James composed himself, then got serious. "I'm trying, Dad. I'm trying to get my life together."

"Does this phone call help or hurt?"

"It helps a lot," James said sincerely. "More than you'll ever know."

With a breaking voice, Chuck said, "It wasn't easy to call, after all these years, James."

"I know, Dad, and I'm sorry for not going to Mom's funeral. Really, really sorry. . . . I miss her so much."

James listened as his father struggled to regain his composure.

"I'm married again . . . to Margaret," Chuck finally said.

"I know. I talked to her a few days ago."

"She's a wonderful person," Chuck said brightly.

"I could tell. I'd like to meet her."

"Uh-huh." Chuck softly blew his nose. "I hear you've got a book published."

"Yes, a book of poetry."

"How's it selling?"

"Um, pretty well, I think. People seem to like it."

"I'll have to pick one up." Chuck paused, then added, "And how's Molly?"

"Good. She lives in Victor, Montana . . . er, at least she did. Her house was gutted by the fire. She's decided to move back to Michigan to teach there."

"And you're in Coeur d'Alene, Idaho, right?"

"Yes."

"So, what are you gonna do about Molly?"

"What do you mean?"

"You said you were trying to get your life back together, so how does Molly fit in?"

James chuckled uneasily. "Well, she's back in my life, but it's a long story. Maybe Molly and I can come out together and tell it to you in person."

"We're in Orlando, and we like it here. Come and visit anytime, if you want."

Tears blurred James's eyes at the unexpected invitation. "Definitely. Thanks."

"OK, Son, I'll let you go."

The word *son* knocked James for a loop. His heart melted, and he fought back tears. "OK, Dad," he said, choking up. "Thanks for calling."

"All right, then. Good-bye."

James grabbed a short breath. "Dad?" he hurried.

"Yeah?"

"I . . . love you."

There was a momentary hush. Then Chuck whispered, "Me too."

James hung up the phone and fell back into bed. *I'm coming back to life!* he exalted, releasing tears of joy.

CHAPTER TWENTY-NINE

Ready for the Journey

Five days later, wearing a western-style suit and cowboy boots with his wig and a new cowboy hat, James arrived at Woody's Books for his book signing, as did more than a hundred other people. Molly and Stephanie were there, along with Wayne Summers and Eric Maclellan, who lifted James's spirits by telling him he looked "real fine." Kelly, obviously happy to have her master back, watched all the hoopla from beneath a table at James's feet. Cupid appeared with some of his street pals, with the express purpose of cheering up everyone. Even Phil Kline and Tom Hathaway called on the phone to wish James and Molly well.

Any repulsion people had to James's war injuries seemed to be overcome by their attraction to him as a successful poet. All were anxious to shake his hand and talk to him. Many had glowing words of praise, having already read James's book of poems.

James realized that people were treating him far nicer than they undoubtedly would have at a chance meeting on the street, but that was OK with him. His heart had changed, so his perspective had changed. He knew he could live a better, more open life from now on. His hope that his poetry might restore some of his self-esteem had been fulfilled, and he had discovered God-esteem through the Bible that Molly had given him.

He touched the lump made by the little Bible inside his suitcoat pocket just after the last poetry book had been autographed and the party had ended. At that moment, Molly walked up and put an arm around his shoulder.

"What a wonderful day!" she gushed, giving him a kiss on the cheek. Then she handed him her copy of *Glimpses of Love and*

Life. "One more, James, before Stephanie and I have to go. It's mine."

James took the book, opened the cover, and wrote for a minute. Giving it back to Molly, he said, "Read it on the way home, OK?"

"Yes," Molly said. "I've got something for you too." She dug the diamond engagement ring out of her purse.

"I want you to keep this," she told him. "If God is in this, maybe you'll be able to put it back on my finger someday."

James slipped the ring into his pants pocket, working at a smile. "Believe me, I long for that day."

James thanked Stephanie for her support and gave her a good-bye hug, knowing her plane was leaving the next morning for Michigan, then he hugged Molly for a long while. When the two pulled apart, each was struck by the sadness in the other's eyes.

"Call me when you get to Missoula so I know you're safe," James told Molly. "I'll be waiting by the phone, so don't forget."

"I won't forget," Molly assured him. "What else is there to do in a motel room? And I'll call you tomorrow night from a friend's house in Victor where I'll be staying for a few weeks."

"That's great."

Molly gave James another hug. "Thanks for saving my life," she whispered in his good ear.

"Thanks for saving mine too," James said happily.

A mile out of Coeur d'Alene, Molly, who was driving the Volvo still packed with her things, asked Stephanie to take the poetry book out of her purse and read James's inscription aloud.

Stephanie got the book and opened the cover. She cleared her throat and read, " 'I have found *love* a second time, and I've found *life* a second time, thanks to you, Molly Meyers. Without your forgiveness and your big heart, I would have nothing. But you, and the Lord, have given me *everything*. Love, James.' "

Closing the cover, Stephanie looked at Molly with tears rimming her eyes. "See," she said, "I *told* you you were big enough."

Molly smiled. "I love you, best friend," she said warmly.

"I love you, Moll, and I always will."

Molly sighed and looked at the road ahead of her. She knew she had a long way to go, but she felt ready for the journey.